I0718797

BEYOND solitude

KIT ROCHA

BEYOND SOLITUDE

Edited by Sasha Knight
Cover Artwork by Bree Bridges

ISBN-13: 978-1-942432-35-7

1

One more drink, and he'd call it a night.

Derek Ford watched the stage intently, cataloging every arch and moan, every flash of bare flesh washed pale by the harsh lights. Shows at the Broken Circle weren't just skin on display, bored dancers humping a pole and counting down the hours until closing. They were real, in-your-face revelries of lust.

And fuck, they were hot. The naked blonde on stage could brew a mean beer, rebuild a carburetor in twenty minutes, and finger her pussy on stage like it was the most fun anyone in the whole goddamn world had ever had. If Ford could manage to remember her name, he might have loved her.

Maybe.

The blonde sucked in a breath and released it on a sharp, shuddering moan, and the crowd lost its collective mind. Cheers erupted and bottles clinked, a perfect representation of Sector Four—packed to the seams with sex and booze, just the way the O'Kanes liked it.

By his own choice, Ford had always existed on the fringes of Dallas O'Kane's gang. He was all in, working his ass off to help secure the group's financial interests. But when it came time to knock off and play, he shied away from some of the more carnal pleasures shared by the other O'Kanes. It wasn't his style.

The blonde rolled to her knees on stage, drawing his attention to the luscious curve of her ass. He shifted in his chair to relieve the pressure caused by the sudden surge of desire—and almost groaned aloud when the ache in his right leg blossomed into fiery pain. It was an immediate and sobering reminder that any and all offers to warm his bed these days were made out of pity, not passion.

Some fucking hero he was.

The redheaded bartender with the mouthwatering rack stopped by his table, her hand lingering over his nearly empty glass. "You want a bottle for the road, Ford?"

Shit, he didn't remember her name, either. It left him casting about for an endearment to cover his forgetfulness. "Yeah, sugar. That'd be real nice."

"You got it."

He followed her to the bar, his stride carefully measured to cover his lingering limp. Doc had assured him he was getting better, that all it took was time and care, but fuck if he could tell the difference sometimes.

Especially when he was tired. He accepted the bottle with thanks and made his way out the door at the back of the room. Through the backstage area, straight to his own personal fucking hell—the steep, narrow stairs leading up to his apartment.

Ford stood at the bottom for a moment, then gritted his teeth as he started walking up. Slow, precise, his right hand clenched around the railing. He clutched the bottle in his left, and halfway up the flight of stairs, he almost lost his grip on some of the best O'Kane whiskey to be found, all because his palms were growing slick and damp with the sweat of exertion.

He heard the sounds before he reached the top, footsteps in his office followed by the clatter of filing cabinets. Someone bit off a curse, a low but feminine sound that made his stomach clench.

Ford swiped his arm across his forehead and flung open the door. A woman stood there, dressed in faded jeans and a halter-top that left a few miles of smooth brown skin bare. Also bare were her wrists, devoid of the tattoos that would have marked her as an O'Kane.

A stranger. She was pretty, built, infinitely fuckable—but she was standing in his home uninvited, and that meant she had to go. "Get out," he growled.

She started at the sound of his voice, clutching a file folder of reports to her chest as she spun around. She tensed, her big brown eyes fixing on his for just a moment before sweeping down to his wrists and *his* tattoos. "Oh," she breathed out. "Are you Ford?"

"Depends on who wants to know."

"Your new assistant." She shuffled the papers to one arm and held out a hand, as damn chipper as if he wasn't standing there glaring at her. "Well, Lex gave me the job, but she said I'd mostly be working with you."

He ignored her proffered hand. "I don't have an assistant. Don't need one."

"No, you have filing cabinets." She frowned and tilted her head. "File cabinets? Honestly, I don't know what they're called or *where* Dallas O'Kane found them. It's barbaric."

Wonderful. Not only had she invaded his personal space, but now she was insulting his organizational skills. "You're a long way from Eden's fancy computers, buttercup. Around here, we make do, even if it involves barbaric pieces of paper for record-keeping."

She braced her free hand on her hip and arched an eyebrow. "Don't tell me the most infamous bootlegger in all eight sectors can't afford a little tech. And I'm *not* from Eden."

No, not with that hint of fire in her eyes. It reached past the throbbing ache in his leg to reignite his banked libido, and he found himself staring at her mouth, waiting for her to lick her lips so he could catch another glimpse of her quick pink tongue.

Ford groaned. The smartest thing would be to scare her off, but she didn't look easily cowed. "I'll pay you to leave," he offered. "How's that?"

Now both of her eyebrows were up. "I don't need a score. I need a *job*. If you don't want me to mess with your files, fine—"

"Okay. Don't mess with my files."

She didn't falter, didn't even blink. "Then tell me what to do instead."

If I were an asshole... He waved the bottle of whiskey at her. "You could start by letting me drink half of this and jerk off so I can get some sleep."

That snapped her teeth together—for about five seconds. "If you're self-conscious about doing that with me in the next room, I could take some work home."

"Self-conscious?" He dropped the bottle on his desk and unbuckled his belt. "I'll lay it out right here, buttercup, if you like to watch."

Her gaze flicked to his hands, and he got that flash

of tongue he'd been waiting for as she wet her lips. "I wouldn't be watching. I'd be working."

Filing papers like there was nothing more interesting going on? Fuck that. "Bullshit." Ford tugged open the top button on his jeans. "It may be a little battered these days, like the rest of me, but my ego's not dead. If I start stroking my dick right in front of you, you're damn sure gonna be paying attention. Not just watching—*riveted*."

The folder in her hands bent under the force of her grip. Not fear though, and that flush in her cheeks wasn't shyness, either. There was too much awareness in her eyes, like she was imagining his cock and how it would look with his hand wrapped around it.

Or maybe *her* hand.

She pivoted abruptly and dumped the crumpled files on his desk. "Life's funny sometimes, isn't it?"

"Goddamn hilarious." He left his belt hanging open, left that one lone button undone, and reached for the whiskey. "What's your name?"

She ignored the question and gestured to his straining fly. "Do you want me to help? Or just watch?"

The thrill of anticipation that shot through him made him the worst kind of asshole, after all. A snake. He snorted to cover it. "If I wanted a whore, lady, I know where to find one. I'm a big boy. I don't need Lex to deliver."

Her expression didn't change, but that damn shirt left her back and shoulders naked, and he could see her muscles tensing. "Lex warned me you were cranky. But calling me a whore won't scare me off, you know. I don't consider it an insult."

Her tone raked at him—defiant and resigned, all at once—and suddenly he knew. "Shit, you're from Two. What house? You act like a Rose."

That made her flinch, though her lips twisted into a mockery of a smile. "Why, because I'm not like Lex? No one's like Lex. A Rose would have blushed and pretended she didn't know what your dick did, because that's what men want, isn't it? A girl who acts like she's never seen a cock but can still swallow it when you shove it down her throat."

That sounded about right—for the fancy men in Two, the ones who liked their women mindless and obedient. Completely dependent, subservient—which was why they all kept whores. "Look, lady, you don't know me or my dick. And Lex didn't give you nearly enough information if you think the men in Sector Four prize bullshit fake innocence over a woman who honestly loves to fuck."

"Fake innocence was never my specialty." She slapped a hand down on the folders. "*This* was. Because Orchid House trains girls to use their brains. That's why Lex is the queen of your damn sector, and why I wanted to work for her."

"And she stuck you here." He snorted again. "That must suck."

"Not hardly. So you're grumpy and drunk and like to talk about your dick." She stepped closer, and he could smell her perfume now—something sensual and floral that hit him low in the gut. "You don't own me. Makes you the best boss I've ever had."

"Give me time, buttercup." He offered her the bottle with one upraised brow.

She snatched the bottle, knocked back a swig— and choked. Furious color returned to her cheeks as her eyes watered, but she managed to swallow around her sputtering. Her gaze found his, and Lord, she was embarrassed as fuck.

Her jaw tightened, and she lifted the bottle again.

Her lips closed around it so slow and deliberate it was fucking well obscene, and she watched him as she took another sip.

She knew what she was doing, all right—and he was playing right into her sweet little hands. "Tomorrow," he murmured finally. "You want to get your hands all over my files? Ten a.m., and don't be late or I'll fire your ass."

Her sudden, radiant smile lit up her face and eyes as she handed the bottle back to him. "Mia. That's my name."

Oh *fuck*. Her fire was one thing, but that smile... It hit him in places more dangerous than his gut, lower and higher. Places he could ill afford for anyone to touch.

He swallowed and nodded. "Got it. Now can you do something for me, Mia?"

"Sure."

"Get out. Seriously."

She smiled again and turned to retrieve her thin jacket. "I'll see you in the morning."

She left, looking pleased with herself, and why shouldn't she? She'd gotten exactly what she wanted, all because he hadn't been able to look into those dark, dark eyes and tell her to get lost.

Ford groaned and dropped into his desk chair. It smelled like flowers now, damn it, the same erotic perfume Mia wore. It wrapped around him, cutting through the sheer relief of being off his injured leg. Instead, tension twisted, leaving his balls heavy—and everything else painfully tight. Achy.

He winced as he pulled open the remaining buttons on his fly and freed his cock. He touched it lightly at first, the way a timid virgin would, then grinned as he shifted his hand to grip his shaft.

Mia wasn't a virgin. And he'd seen one thing in her eyes as her gaze had traveled over him—she wanted to touch him.

She wanted it bad.

She wouldn't hesitate to take what she wanted, either. Ford closed his eyes, and the image came immediately—Mia, on her knees, walking her fingers slowly up his thighs. He groaned and squeezed his hand for a moment before relaxing into easy strokes. Not too fast, not at first.

His mind formed the words, whispered them as instructions to the Mia in his fantasy, and his pulse stuttered as his own hands disobeyed...just like she undoubtedly would. He bit off a curse and thumbed the head of his dick, slicking through the moisture his raw arousal had already released.

He opened his eyes, dragged open the top drawer on the right side of his desk, and retrieved the small bottle of lube he kept there. It was cool as he poured it out in his palm, and Ford hissed when he wrapped his hand around his erection once again.

The whiskey beckoned, and he lifted the bottle to his lips. He could taste Mia on the glass, and he groaned as he began to pump into his hand, quick and hard. He could fuck her like this, with her long, smooth legs over the arms of his chair, her tits just out of reach of his mouth. He'd hold her hips above his and drive up into her—

He squeezed his fist as the first pulses of pleasure tickled down his spine, and he came with breathless speed, silent as he swallowed another groan. No, not a groan—a word—

Mia.

2

Mia woke up on a thin mattress in a narrow bed, staring at a paint-cracked ceiling as it shuddered beneath the trampling steps of her upstairs neighbor. The wall beside her head was just as shabby and insubstantial. The girl who rented the room next door was already up and singing some pre-Flare classic, high and off-key, every word as audible as if she were perched at Mia's table.

Her apartment was a dingy little room in a sad little building, with everyone scraping by on stolen power and water that never heated beyond tepid. Her furniture was fifth-hand, sagging and patched, and the landlord was horrid, stooped and mean and threatening to raise Mia's rent every time she turned around.

She'd fallen so far from the luxury of Sector Two that she could hardly credit it, and Mia still smiled as she crawled out of bed.

No more gilded cages for her. No more trading her dignity for silken sheets, or her pride for comfortable surroundings. No more late nights huddled in the bathtub, trying to scrub away the hurtful words, as if water and soap could make her feel clean on the inside. Her heart and soul weren't for sale anymore.

Neither was her body.

Oh, it had been tempting. She'd almost done it a dozen times during that first disorienting week. She could have walked into the fanciest whorehouse in Sector Four and presented her credentials, and there would have been no cold baths or dirty floors. Just comfort, familiar luxury, and the game she'd been learning to play since the day her parents sold her to Orchid House in desperate hopes of giving her a better life. Please the men. Make them feel good, invincible. Lie to them.

But she was tired of telling men what they wanted to hear. If the first week had been overwhelming, the next two had taught her that. She was still drunk on the freedom to do and say what she wanted. She didn't have to please anyone but herself. She didn't *want* to.

At least, she hadn't before last night.

Not that Ford wanted a whore. He'd made that painfully clear, somewhere in between opening his belt and invading her dreams. And he'd guessed she was from Two as if it were branded on her forehead. *Damaged goods* or *broken toy* or whatever men like him thought of girls like her.

She hated that she'd responded to him, that the frank crudeness in his gaze had stirred a response in her body. But he'd *seen* her, and his words—

Lex didn't give you nearly enough information if you think the men in Sector Four prize bullshit fake innocence over a woman who honestly loves to fuck. No, if Derek Ford ever fucked his own fist while calling her a dirty girl, he would mean it as a compliment.

It was wrong to close her eyes and imagine it, but even the lukewarm bath water couldn't stop her entirely. He'd gotten hard last night. He'd stood there unashamedly erect, his belt undone, that top button popped open like a challenge. Lex had said he was struggling to recover from a near-fatal motorcycle accident, but Mia had seen no hint of weakness as he'd loomed over her, all broad shoulders and dark hair and eyes so bottomless they defined *brooding*.

And he'd still been fully clothed, all except for that button. That goddamn *button*. Thinking about it made her mouth water, her fingers itch. If she'd taken a few more sips of the liquor, she might have begged to slide down his body and try all the things her patron had never let her do to him. All the things the good people of Eden would call a sin, as if the word had any meaning in a world that had ended before Mia's parents had even been born.

She dumped cold water over her head to rinse her hair and wash away all her sinful thoughts, then scurried out of the tub as her teeth began to chatter. The air was just as chilly in her apartment, so she hurried into her last clean outfit and her borrowed coat and boots.

Everything she had was charity, including the wad of cash nestled in a box on her rickety table. But she still peeled off five precious bills, enough to buy breakfast and tea for two in the marketplace near the O'Kane compound. A peace offering, because she could hear her trainer's voice droning in her head. *You catch more flies with honey, Mia. Why must you persist in being vinegar?*

Because she'd never wanted to catch flies before.

She stroked her finger over the locket nestled beside her money before closing the box and rushing out of her apartment. The key stuck in the lock until she jiggled it and lifted the door, but in a minute she was down the narrow stairs and out into the dirty street.

The sun was already up, flooding the alley with clear, cool light, but the cracked sidewalk in front of her building was still lined with men huddled around the fires they'd built in huge metal drums. They exchanged cigarettes and flasks and watched her as she shoved her hands deep into her jacket pockets and strode determinedly past them.

"Hey, sweets. Need a man to keep you warm?" one of them called after her, his voice edged with a meanness she recognized all too well. She ignored him and walked faster, lifting her gaze to the tall wall that separated the pristine city of Eden from the dirty tangle of humanity struggling to survive on this side.

The closer you got to the walls, the nicer things were—but they were expensive, too. It was a ten-minute walk to the O'Kane compound, through narrow streets lined with hard-faced men and women who eyed her shabby, patched coat and worn boots and probably judged her not worth the trouble of robbing.

Probably.

One sharp-eyed woman paused to do a double take, and Mia ducked between two men and hopped up onto the sidewalk, doing her best to project confidence. One of the first lessons any girl in Orchid House learned was that predators could sense fear—and that they were being molded into perfect, tempting prey.

Perfect, tempting traps.

She made it safely to the street that led to the O'Kane compound and walked another five blocks to the edge of the marketplace. One vendor had a clock on his stall that read half past nine, so she hurried to the stand that sold luscious pastries baked fresh in the little shop behind the table.

She smiled at the plump, pretty woman managing the sales, and tucked some extra money into her hand after accepting the paper sack. "Can I rent one of the thermoses for the tea, Pam?"

"Not drinking it in the shop this morning, honey?"

Mia had every day for the last week, borrowing the warmth her apartment didn't have and trading lighthearted stories with Pam and her husband. But today would be different. Today would be the start of a whole lot of differences. "No, I've got a new job that starts in twenty minutes. The boss already told me I'm fired if I'm late."

Laughing, Pam poured tea into a battered tin thermos, the kind with a plastic cup that twisted off the top. "You found a job already? I bet Lou you would. You look like a clever girl."

She *was* a clever girl, but that violated another of the trainer's rules. *Everyone likes to make use of a woman's brains, but no one wants to be forced to admit she has them.* So she smiled and demurred with a shrug. "It's nothing fancy. Just doing paperwork for the O'Kanes."

Mia had seen too many fixed smiles not to realize the other woman had gone stiff. Her smile was still there, but it was forced now. She twisted the top onto the thermos and pushed it across the counter. Uncertain, Mia wrapped her chilled hands around the blessedly warm metal, only to find folded cash being stuffed beneath her fingers.

"You have a good day at work," Pam said intently, patting Mia's hand. "No need for the deposit, love. Just return it when you have a chance. Or come back tomorrow, and we'll refill it. We know where our loyalties lie."

"All right," Mia agreed, mostly to soothe the anxiety in the older woman's gaze. She lifted her bag with one last smile and slipped back into the crowd, making it two blocks before she was safely out of view and could look at the cash in her hand.

It was all there. Not just the money for the container—*all* of it.

God, if the mere mention of Dallas O'Kane's name garnered this sort of treatment, no wonder the people who wore his ink around their wrists wandered through the most dangerous parts of the sector with impunity. She could get used to that kind of reflected power.

The market was only a stone's throw from the four square blocks that housed the O'Kane compound. Mia crossed the parking lot behind the Broken Circle and climbed the stairs with fifteen minutes to spare. Remembering Ford's anger at finding his office invaded the previous night, she didn't shove through the door.

She knocked.

"Come in," came the gruff reply.

Better than *go the fuck away*. Taking it as an optimistic sign, Mia slipped through the door and held the bag in front of her like a white flag of truce. "I brought fresh cinnamon rolls."

Ford barely glanced up from the sheaf of papers in his hand. "I already ate."

He was wearing a T-shirt today, a plain cotton thing that should have been unremarkable—though she supposed the remarkable part was how it hugged everything beneath it. It took supreme effort to drag her gaze from his powerful chest to the tousled, dark hair curling damply against his neck.

Oh, he was enchanting. Grumpy and rude and beautiful and so, so much fun to look at.

There was a folding chair propped against the door, its message clear—she might be tolerated, but she wouldn't be welcome.

Grumpy, indeed.

Hiding a smile, she shifted the bag and thermos to one arm and grabbed the chair. "I hope you don't mind if I eat. I'll be quick."

He frowned at her. "Your hair is wet."

"So is yours," she replied easily. It took a little maneuvering, but she managed to unfold the chair with one hand and her knee.

"I haven't been outside in the bitter cold."

Better not to tell him how cold her bath had been, then. The chair was wobbly, but sturdier than the one in her apartment. She settled in and savored the sweet smell of spice and sugar as she opened her breakfast. "It's nice and warm in your office. I'll be thawed out in no time."

But Ford only grunted. "Dry your hair before you come to work," he instructed. "I'm not taking the time to train you if you're only going to up and die on me."

She spared a wistful thought for the hair dryer she'd taken for granted in Sector Two. Even if she could find one in the market that cost less than a week's pay, who knew if she'd have the electricity to run it on any given morning?

Obstacles are opportunities to hone your wits. Her trainer had a pithy saying for any occasion, but that one was true enough. Give her a few weeks with Ford and her wits would be sharp enough to cut steel. "All right. What do you want me to look at first?"

He slid a folder across the desk. "Grain suppliers. We used to import directly as well as through other sectors—Three, specifically. I've been working on taking all of our deals straight to the source."

Her interest piqued, Mia pushed her bag aside and reached for the folder. "You mean the farms? I admit I wondered where you obtained your grain. It can't just be from the communes. Eden keeps a chokehold on the reserves."

He lifted one strong shoulder in a casual shrug. "It's my job to loosen that hold. Not too much, but enough."

She scanned the list of suppliers and reconciled it with her mental dossier of Eden's official farming communes and some of the larger illegal operations. "You don't have the South Tahoe Collective on here."

"You know your shit, I'll give you that." A muscle in Ford's jaw clenched. "We don't deal with Tahoe. Dallas doesn't like the way they operate."

Neither did he, that much was clear from his narrowed eyes and compressed lips. She didn't blame him. The one time her patron had hosted a representative from Tahoe, she'd endured two straight days of leering and "accidental" groping, and the cruel edge in the man's eyes had left her with no doubt what would happen if she let him catch her alone.

And he'd tried. He'd tried everything up to slipping into her bedroom, and on the final night of his visit he'd tried that too, foiled only by her locked door. She reported the attempt to Vaughn the next morning, expecting her patron to at least resent the insult to his pride if not the threat to her safety, but he'd brushed her off with the cold words that had been the beginning of the end of her life in Sector Two. *If you'd done your duty when he first arrived, he wouldn't have been reduced to such theatrics.*

So many things wrong with that statement. So many fucking things, but the worst was that, for a moment, she'd almost believed him.

Ford flipped the folder shut. "We rotate through suppliers, for two reasons. One, it helps ensure they're not overtaxed. Secondly..."

Mia dragged her attention back to the cluttered safety of Ford's office. He'd trailed off with a slightly raised eyebrow, as if testing her, so she scrambled to reconstruct what he'd been saying. "You can't afford to give any one supplier that much power over the future of your business."

"Very good. Maybe you can help me, after all."

Yes, sometimes girls have brains, too. She bit her lip against the words, because there was no point in them. A woman didn't get to tell a man she was smart. She had to prove she was smart, and then prove it wasn't a fluke, and God help her if she seemed proud of her accomplishments.

A clever woman convinces a man her idea has merit. An Orchid convinces a man her idea was his all along.

She'd only been free of Sector Two for three weeks. Too soon for a lifetime of lessons to slip away, but she hoped her trainer's voice went first. All those lessons cautioning her not to be too bright, too eager, too open, too* real...*

Fuck the lessons. By the time she was done tearing through Derek Ford's life, he wouldn't know how he'd ever made it a day without her. She could reach as high as she wanted here—Lex was proof of that. She'd fled Orchid House, had worked her way up to stand as

Dallas O'Kane's partner and the queen of Sector Four.

Mia didn't need to be royalty, but she would damn sure have Ford's respect by the end of the month. And maybe warm water and steady electricity, too.

And a damn hair dryer.

3

He had to hand it to her, the girl was doing a damn good job.

It had taken her only an hour or so to go through the files, sort them, and begin scanning them into the system Noah had already programmed. Of course, she'd raised an eyebrow at the sight of the optical character recognition scanner, and it was plain to see that kind of tech was the last thing she'd expected to find in Sector Four.

It was unsettling to discover how much he delighted in surprising her.

She was frowning now, dragging her finger down a shipment inventory list. "It's more complicated than I realized. I've been trying to reconcile a pattern in which grains you get in what quantities and when, but it seems completely random."

"Supply and demand, buttercup. We have to take deals when we can get them. Plus, I never know what Nessa will need for her smaller batches."

Mia twisted to reach for the tablet she'd commandeered. The hem of her sweater hiked up, baring a glimpse of luscious skin. "I saw something about those. A rebranding plan?"

He averted his gaze. "More like extending the O'Kane brand. Nessa's been developing some special liquors—older ones, aging in special casks, that sort of thing. No way could she make enough to meet general demand, and no way could some asshole off the street pay for it. But there's always someone who will, if only so he can show everyone else how much better he is."

She made an amused little noise. "So, most of the men in Sector Two."

"Not just Two." He hesitated, then forged ahead. She might as well know. "Other sectors, as well. Eight, for example. That's where I'm from."

"Oh?" Her gaze flicked up to his. "Did you work at one of the factories?"

"Not exactly. I worked for Jim Jernigan."

"So you've always been an important man." Her full lips tugged up. "That explains a lot."

"I wasn't important enough to keep around." But important enough to get rid of. One thing hadn't changed over the years, and that was Jernigan's ruthless pragmatism. Smart men were useful...up to a point.

O'Kane was different. He didn't throw people away out of fear or boredom, and suddenly Ford needed her to know that.

Except he didn't know how to say it, so he said nothing.

She tilted her head, her smile fading. "I never

met Jernigan. Vau—my patron, he wasn't prominent enough to be meeting with sector heads, or even the more reputable communes. Which is probably for the best now."

"Because he can't come get you?"

"I don't think he would, unless he wanted a refund." She wrinkled her nose and stared down at the tablet. "But if he had more influence, he might send people after me. Or get my House to do it."

For a moment, she looked lost, and Ford steeled himself against the urge to comfort her. "You're in Sector Four now. Dallas is king here."

"And Lex is queen." Mia spoke the name with a reverence that probably would have made Lex laugh. But it seemed to bolster her confidence as she reached for the scanner. "Just the same, if anyone comes looking for me, maybe you could say you've never heard of me?"

It was a joke, but it wasn't funny. "You work for the O'Kanes. Surely you've seen how things run by now. You're protected."

Her gaze jumped to the thermos, where it sat abandoned on the edge of his desk with her forgotten breakfast. "Lex didn't really explain. If something happens..."

"If someone hassles you, you mean?" The mere thought made his hands clench into fists.

"I'm not a martyr, but I'm not helpless either. I can handle a little hassle. But if it's serious, should I tell someone?"

If it was serious, she shouldn't have to. Ford made a mental note to ask around. "Lex can handle it. Or you can come to me."

She nodded and changed the subject as she initiated the next scan. "I could get through all of these if I stay late tonight. Do you mind?"

"Not a good idea, unless you're willing to have someone escort you home."

Her lips pressed together, but he couldn't decipher her expression. "Tomorrow, then. If you can spare a tablet, I'll proof the extracted data tonight instead."

She probably wanted to spare his lame ass the trek across the sector. Or, worse, she considered him piss-poor personal protection against whatever threats might await her. "It wouldn't be me," he offered. "We can get one of the bouncers in the club. Zan, maybe."

"No, it's okay. Maybe I'll find a place closer to the compound, so no one will have to worry about walking me." She tossed him another bright, cheerful smile, so out of place in the sectors. "Now that I know the land-lords won't cheat me if I tell them who I work for."

It was none of his business. Ford repeated the refrain as he gathered some of the completed documents and rose. His leg ached, stiff and sore from sitting for too long, and he gritted his teeth as he braced one arm on the desk.

She hopped to her feet and swept up another stack. "Here, I can take those. It'll be good practice."

"I've got it," he barked.

Mia stared him down for a few seconds, worrying at her lower lip with her teeth. "Lex said you were in an accident."

Ford squeezed his eyes shut. None of it seemed real, even weeks after the fact. The screech of metal, the blazing pain. The long, delirious hours spent drifting in and out of consciousness through the blazing heat of day and the chill of night.

The blood.

"There's not much to tell," he heard himself say calmly. "Crashed my bike, broke my leg. By the time I made my way back to town, infection had set in. That's it, the whole tragic fucking story. Anything else you want to know?"

Her eyes had gone wide. "You *walked* back?"

The way she was looking at him made him shift uncomfortably. "What else was I supposed to do, lie there and die?"

"No, but..." She shivered. "That's incredible. Not that you tried. That you made it. I understand going down fighting, but most of us don't get back up."

It was the perfect opportunity to take advantage of her starry expression. He could spin it out like a yarn, boast about how easy it had been. How it was nothing for a hero like him.

Instead, harsh words came. "It was hell. Sometimes, I'm still not sure why I bothered."

"Because it gets better."

She said it with such hope, and Ford opened his mouth to agree with her. But what came out was anything but comforting. "Not always, buttercup. Lesson number one in the sectors—sometimes what's broken stays broken."

The light went out of her.

Not all at once. He had to watch it die in stages, her eyes dulling, her shoulders slumping. She finally looked away and extended her hand to him blindly. "I'll file the papers."

"Fine." Guilt sharpened his tone. "Suit yourself."

No reply. She took the work from him and moved to the filing cabinets in silence. She'd been yammering constantly since her arrival, but no more. Now she was stony. Cold.

Well, what do you expect, jackass? She'd been looking for a little hope, and he'd crushed it ruthlessly under his boot. Never mind that he'd been talking about himself, not her. The end result was the same.

But apologizing was out of the question, because she might start thinking he gave a damn. So he kept his mouth shut and hobbled off, leaving her to her work.

Mia hadn't realized how fragile her grip on hope was until Ford sent it spinning away.

The dreary trudge back to her apartment took forever, and she noticed *everything*. The garbage in the streets, the menace of strangers watching from the growing shadows, even the bitter wind slicing through the spots where her jacket was worn thin. Small blessing that only a few men had gathered around the trashfire in front of her apartment, and they all seemed too intent on the flask they were passing around to call lewd suggestions to her.

Her adventure had gone sour, and she would make Derek Ford pay for stealing it from her.

Tomorrow.

As if to add insult to injury, the power flickered as she reached the second floor. It cast the hallway into near-darkness, broken only when the landlady threw open her door. She had power, of course, undoubtedly supplied by the generator humming in the background.

Bracing herself for another battle over rent, Mia stepped into the rectangle of light. "Mrs. Jones."

"Mia." Gone was the woman's customary derisive glare. She kept her gaze downcast, deferential. "You had a delivery today."

Mia had almost forgotten how true terror felt. Like ice in her guts while her nerves misfired, seizing every muscle with the animal instinct to run, to flee for her fucking life. But she hadn't forgotten how to hide it. Her smile felt brittle as she lifted one brow in a poor imitation of curiosity. "Oh? I wasn't expecting anything."

"I let him put it in your apartment. One of O'Kane's men, it was."

Oxygen returned. Exhaling roughly, Mia forced her muscles to relax. Not that it wasn't unsettling to realize her landlady would let anyone wearing O'Kane ink into an apartment that was supposed to be private...

But it could have been worse. It could have been *so* much worse.

"I'm sure that's fine, then," she said, digging her keys out of her pocket. "I'm sorry if they put you out."

"It's no bother," the old lady protested. "You tell them anyone is welcome to stop by. Any time, okay? I've got nothing to hide here."

Caught in the awkward position of comforting a woman who'd been haranguing her twenty-four hours earlier, Mia managed a barely believable pat on the arm...and took shameless advantage of her new status. "I'll let him know," she promised, careful not to indicate who *he* might be. Let the old bat imagine she sat down to morning tea with Dallas O'Kane.

At least it would keep her rent low.

"You do that. And, uh, let me know if there's anything you need."

The woman was following her down the hallway, so eager to please, and Mia was beginning to understand why Ford had seemed so outraged at the suggestion that someone would hassle an employee of the O'Kanes. Unless excessive obsequiousness counted as hassle.

She shoved the key into the sticky lock and wiggled it until the deadbolt released. "I will, Mrs. Jones. Have a good night."

"You too, Mia. And remember what I said about—"

Mia closed the door and only felt a little guilty about it.

The light from her one barred window had already faded, but hopefully there had been plenty of sunlight during the day. She traversed the room carefully, catching up her unlit lantern on her way past the table.

Her most valuable possession—a tiny solar recharger—lay on the windowsill. Not a very nice one, since it took a full day of strong sunlight to power her lantern for a few hours, but it was better than spending her night in the dark.

She fit the battery into place by touch and was rewarded with a bright, cheerful spill of light. Her apartment was so small it reached all but the farthest corners, which meant it didn't take long to realize what was out of place.

The "delivery" sat in the corner between her mattress and bathtub, narrow and boxy, with vents on the front, a neat row of buttons...and no power cord. She brushed her finger over the power button and almost yelped in surprise when blessedly warm air gusted over her.

One of O'Kane's men had shown up, bullied his way past her terrified landlady, and left her a battery-powered space heater.

Utterly perplexed, she picked up the folded piece of paper resting on the top.

The battery should last twelve hours on high power. You can recharge it at work.

No signature, but she'd been digging through paperwork filled out by Ford all day. It was his handwriting, sparse and neat and abrupt, just like him. A peace offering of his own, maybe, or an easy way of buying out of his guilt at being such an asshole.

Or maybe he really hated wet hair.

"Too bad, Derek Ford," she muttered, dragging the heater closer to her bed. Talking to herself wasn't a good sign, but the gift was. It meant there was something under all that pain and bitterness, even if Ford couldn't see it himself. Something she could find if she pushed hard enough, something she could make him remember.

He was wounded, lashing out at anyone who witnessed his moments of supposed weakness, as if someone who'd walked a dozen miles on a broken leg could be *weak*. God must have put men on the Earth with a surplus of social advantages because it was their only hope of surviving their incapacitating egos.

She was a damn Orchid. Not exactly an accomplished one, but even the rawest initiate ate delicate male ego for breakfast. Starting tomorrow, she would embrace the stubbornness that had gotten her this far, as well as the skills that had kept her alive.

Derek Ford could be as hopeless as he wanted. She'd fucking well hope enough for the both of them.

4

The damn man never had any good news.

Dylan Jordan slipped on a pair of glasses and peered down at the open folder in front of him. By the time he raised his head, he wore an expression of utter disgust. "I don't care what the hell you want, Ford, we can't try the regeneration therapy again. With infections like yours—"

"I understand all that," Ford replied. "But you said my infection was under control. No fevers, no nothing. My wounds are all healed."

"That's not the only reason we can't do it. Look, I could explain it all to you, but it's complicated and you really don't give a shit about the particulars. You only care if it works, right?"

Ford couldn't argue. "So I'm stuck, then. Med-gel isn't an option, and neither is regen."

"But you're healing," the man said with uncharacteristic gentleness. "You're healing the way people did for thousands of years before we had this technology. Slowly but surely."

It takes time. "I know, I know. It's just..."

"Hard, yeah." Doc hesitated. "I'm sorry. Truly, I am."

A knock rattled the door, mere seconds before one of the newer girls, Jade, stuck her head inside. Doc straightened at the sight of her, abruptly dragging his spectacles from his face.

Ford rolled his eyes. "What's up, Jade?"

She was the sort of gorgeous that didn't seem quite real, like one of the pre-Flare paintings Ace collected in his studio. Her voice was warm and breathy, and all for Doc. "Dylan, I didn't realize you were here."

"I, uh, came by to see Ford. And I was just leaving." He rose and gathered his bag from the floor beside his chair, then leveled a serious gaze on Ford. "If you need anything..."

"I'll be fine, Doc. See you next week."

Jade murmured her goodbyes, watching until the door swung shut behind the doctor. When she turned back to Ford, he didn't get the sweet, honeyed smiles and gentle whispers.

No, he got hands on the hips and a disapproving frown. "You vex him, you know."

"Vex?" The word almost made him laugh. "We can't have that, can we? Not when you're so sweet on him."

"You're very good at deflection. I'm not surprised you're so successful in business."

"You're a sweet talker, Jade." Ford leaned back in his chair and held his hands out wide. "So, what can I do for you?"

She relented, giving the folding chair a dubious look before sinking gracefully onto it. "I came to see how Mia was settling in."

"Fine." He couldn't keep the slight tinge of defensiveness from his voice, and he damned himself for it. The woman sitting across his desk was from Sector Two, same as Mia—same as *Lex*—and she would hear every word he didn't say.

Sure enough, she studied him for a silent moment before tilting her head. "That's good. You have no idea how relieved I was when I heard she'd reached out for help. She was always such a smart girl, utterly wasted on that..." Her lips pressed together tightly.

"Her patron wasn't the most pleasant man, I take it?" Not that Ford cared, obviously. He didn't.

Jade seemed to weigh her words. "Lex casts a long shadow over Sector Two," she said finally. "Especially over Orchid House. Cerys likes girls with brains, but the ones who show too much spirit... Well, she'd rather see them a little broken than have another Lex out here working against her."

A chill slithered up his spine. "If that were Mia's situation, Cerys never would have let her go. I know that much."

"You're assuming Cerys knows she's gone." Jade met his gaze squarely. "I may be borrowing trouble, Ford. God knows I have reason to see malice and ill intent in everything Cerys does. She won't move against Dallas openly, but we both know that doesn't make Mia safe."

She had wreathed the words in a carefully casual tone, but Ford wasn't stupid. They were a warning, pure and simple. "So what do we need to do?"

"Make her feel welcome. Make her feel valued." Her jaw tightened, a tiny physical clue to the sudden fury in her eyes. "And if that disgusting excuse for a patron shows up in the sector looking for her, find an excuse to kill him."

Ford rose, drawing himself up to his full, considerable height. "This is Sector Four," he said grimly. "I don't need a fucking excuse."

Ford had gotten her a new chair.

Mia eyed it as she set her thermos down on the edge of the massive desk. It wasn't fancy, but it was sturdy and padded. Ford didn't say anything about it— he didn't even look up from whatever he was writing— so Mia let herself smile. "Good morning."

He grunted.

Poor, grumpy Ford. Schooling her features into a mask of cheerful innocence, Mia unbuttoned her coat. "Do you like my new hat? My landlady was waiting with it when I left this morning. I think she was up all night knitting it."

"Must have figured out who you worked for." He finally lifted his head, only to tap his pen on the desk. "You need a new coat, too. When it warms up, we'll go to the market."

Not *would you like a new coat?*, and no acknowledgment of how her landlady had come by that knowledge. She was starting to get the measure of him now, even if it formed an inexplicable picture. What sort of man wasted time and effort on a woman without wanting appreciation and gratitude in return?

A wounded one. Her chest aching with sympathy, she hung up her jacket and tried to keep her voice light. "I don't know if that's a good idea. There are about five people on my walk home who are already considering robbing me for this one."

He turned his attention back to his writing. "Not after we make a big production of parading around the marketplace, there won't be."

In his world maybe it really was that simple. A woman only had to be seen with him once to be safe throughout the sector, and that was seductive in dangerous ways. Power was attractive for a reason. You could curl up close to it and bask in security, in the warmth and safety...

Until it went wrong. And then no one could help you. No one dared.

Mia tugged her new chair closer to the desk and sank into it. "It's sweet of you to offer, but that's not what I plan to spend my first week's wages on. And you can't go buying me any more presents."

"Don't argue with me. And it's not a gift. Consider it a job benefit."

Maybe she wasn't a smart girl after all, because anyone with wits would have fallen into obedient silence. This was the job of a damn lifetime. Good pay, constant gifts, spending her days staring at a beautiful, brooding hulk of a man. She should be wary of him. Respectful.

She shouldn't want to keep poking just to see if he'd snap. But Vaughn had been oblivious to her presence, even staring right at her. The only emotion she'd ever stirred in him had been self-loathing. He hadn't wanted to find her desirable, and he'd hated her for holding that power over him.

Ford's attention—his *focus*—prickled over her skin, though he'd done his best to ignore her.

The silence had stretched on too long. She almost let it go, but the urge was too strong to resist. Leaning across the desk, she lowered her voice to a whisper. "I think you like it when I argue with you."

He froze, his gaze slowly tracking up until his eyes locked with hers. "I've been through worse."

Goose bumps rose in a shivering wave, and she found herself studying his lips. They were firm, wide. She'd never kissed a man before, but she hadn't thought it would be much different from kissing women. Maybe it wasn't, always, but kissing him would be. His stubble would rasp against her chin, her cheeks. It would rasp against any sensitive place his lips wandered.

If they wandered. He might be abrupt and hurried, hoisting her onto the desk and working into her with a need that would curl her toes.

Her cheeks felt warm. Her voice, when it came, was almost breathless. "Do you always win arguments?"

The corner of his mouth twitched up. "Sure I do, buttercup. Because I don't have them."

"That's not winning. That's cheating."

"It gets the job done."

Her heart did a funny kick in her chest, and the next words that spilled out weren't idle flirtation, but raw, vulnerable bafflement. "Why do you care if I have a new coat?"

"I don't." But his sudden, soft smile contradicted his claim. Then he reached up, touched her cheek, and she *knew* he was lying. And she didn't want to move, because nothing had ever felt as full of heavy, beautiful promise as those roughened fingertips brushing over her skin.

"Okay," she breathed, not breaking eye contact. "Okay, I'll take the coat. Thank you."

"Good." His touch vanished as he sat back in his chair. "Your hair is dry this morning. I approve."

It wasn't fair to feel the loss of his fingers on her skin so profoundly. So she hid it, straightening in her chair. "Yes, the heater makes things much more comfortable. If you can figure out how to get me enough hot water for a nice long bath, life would be downright cozy."

"I'll work on it." He dropped his pen and stood. "No scanning or filing today. You want to know what the O'Kanes are all about? Time for you to see."

Excitement surged, all flirting forgotten. This was what she needed more than new clothes and idle touches—a chance to learn enough to prove herself. "You mean the liquor? Because that's what's slowing down my data analysis. I don't understand more than the vague details of how it's made, or how the ingredients impact quality and price."

He walked around the desk, his limp barely noticeable as he strode toward the coat rack by the door. He lifted a battered, soft-looking leather jacket and slid his arms into it. "I don't know how much of that you can glean from a simple tour, but you've got to start somewhere."

"No knowledge is wasted knowledge," she said lightly, rising to retrieve her own jacket.

The words echoed in her head as she followed him out the door. *No knowledge is wasted knowledge.* Not her trainer's voice this time, but Jade's. An unusual sentiment for someone trained as a Rose instead of an Orchid, but there had been nothing usual about the woman Cerys had chosen to exert Sector Two's influence over one of the most prominent councilmen in Eden.

There'd been nothing usual about Jade's spectacular retirement, either. Gossip had raced through Sector Two, claims that her oh-so-important patron was dead and she was missing—and, beneath the gossip, the quiet whispers traded from girl to girl. Whispers that Cerys had allowed the councilman to addict Jade to a drug that made her malleable and would kill her if withheld. That her life had been in danger, and her house had turned a blind eye.

The softest whispers of all passed from Orchid to Orchid, sometimes with condemnation, sometimes with hope, but always with awe. Jade's house had turned a blind eye...but Lex Parrino hadn't.

No wonder Cerys hated the queen of Sector Four. Knowing that Lex existed had given Mia the courage to run.

Ford led her slowly down the stairs. He took them one at a time, setting both feet on each stair before moving on to the next. He gripped the handrail, white-knuckled and careful, but he didn't tremble, and he didn't falter.

He had to be in agony, but she bit her lip and said nothing.

On the first floor, he released a breath and waved her toward a door. "The main room," he supplied as she pushed through it. "The Broken Circle. Aside from exporting liquor, this is Dallas's biggest moneymaker."

It was still early, barely past nine, but the bar wasn't empty. A gorgeous redhead leaned against the bar, checking off notes on a datapad, while a pretty brunette with a familiar face pulled chairs off tables. She turned as the door opened and smiled widely. "Ford! Are you here for breakfast? We have some toast and eggs left."

He shook his head. "Girls, this is Mia. Mia..." He waved a hand toward the bar.

The redhead grinned. "You're especially chipper this morning, Ford. It's a good look for you."

He ignored her in favor of sliding onto a stool at the bar. "Mia's here to get a feel for things."

Mia shot the brunette a furtive glance as she took

the stool next to Ford, trying to picture her without the tattoos, heavy eyeliner, and leather.

Noelle Cunningham had been in all the news vids over the summer, the headline of scandalized stories detailing her fall from Eden royalty, but the pictures they'd flashed of a sweet, demure councilman's daughter had been washed out and pale compared to the vibrant woman who leaned against the bar beside Mia.

There was nothing demure about her smile as she offered her hand. "I'm Noelle. She's Trix. And Ford's terrible at introductions."

"I'm her boss, not her social director."

Mia ignored him and clasped Noelle's hand. "It's nice to meet you."

"Have you eaten?" Noelle didn't give her a chance to respond before pushing away to circle the bar. "Don't take that girl out of here without letting me feed her, Ford!" she called as she disappeared through the swinging doors, and Mia hid a smile by pressing her lips together as hard as she could.

Trix stood there for a moment before taking a step back. "Right. I'm going to help her. Nice to meet you, Mia."

The door swung lazily back into place after she vanished, and Mia snuck a peek at Ford, surprised his habitual frown hadn't reappeared. Not that he was smiling or anything—God forbid—but he seemed mellow, even in the face of Noelle's affectionate teasing.

Interesting. "So I'm starting to think cheating at arguments is an O'Kane thing."

He shrugged one shoulder. "That's the thing about being in a position of power, buttercup. You don't have to fight if you don't want to."

"But she wasn't even fighting with *you*."

"Should she?"

Unless she didn't have any power at all—or had just as much as he did. Hard to fathom a place where women shared the same easy authority as men, but Noelle and Trix had both had the same ink around their wrists as Lex and Ford. "Does she have power?"

"What are you really asking?" Ford reached over the bar, but instead of liquor he picked up a bottle of water. "Noelle is a member. She wears the ink, same as me. Same as anyone else."

"Oh." Only a man could say that as if it should have been obvious, as if it wasn't close to incomprehensible.

Then, just when she thought he really didn't understand how insane all this was, he glanced over at her. "You'll get used to it."

God, she hoped so.

Off balance and desperate to cover it, she rose on her elbows and peered over the bar, taking in the endless row of bottles with their artistic labels. "So this is the stuff you sell here?"

He inclined his head in a nod. "The finest liquor there is."

It couldn't all be fine. As meager as her apartment was, she was doing damn well compared to some of the people around her. Five or ten people often crowded into rooms the size of hers, and if they could afford O'Kane liquor, then some of it had to be dirt cheap.

She picked up the nearest bottle and examined the label. It looked hand drawn, with the O'Kane emblem front and center and intricate lettering beneath declaring it a *Broken Circle Exclusive*. Not time-consuming to produce, if you had a chemical-reaction printer that could mass reproduce a drawing on paper. And the bottles could be recycled, if you could get people to bring them back. "Are the margins good?"

"On the moonshine and rotgut? Outstanding.

Narrows a bit, the higher up the chain you go."

Tucking that bit of knowledge away, she returned the bottle and picked up another. "Which one's your favorite?"

"The O'Kane specialty—the whiskey."

She had to shuffle through a few more bottles to find it. "Is this what you were drinking the other night?"

He grunted in confirmation. "Want to try it?"

There was something teasing under the words, maybe even a challenge. It was damned uncivilized to start drinking the hard stuff before ten in the morning, but wasn't that the point of Sector Four? Vaughn's obsession with civilized behavior had given her no reason to cling to the concept.

A row of clean shot glasses lined the bar, ready for use. She plucked up one and grinned at him. "You think I won't?"

"I think you can't handle it."

Her pride prickled. "How many?"

Ford laughed. "How many what? Shots? Or seconds before you get all woozy and hit the floor?"

"Bet me." She set down the glass and opened the bottle. "How many do I have to do to win?"

He rolled his eyes and blew out a breath, still chuckling. "I don't know, three. Yeah, sure. Three shots."

Three shots might set her to wobbling, but better to find out now, when she still had time to sober up before her walk home. "What do you want if you win?"

Ford braced a hand on the bar. The muscles in his arm and shoulder flexed as he pushed himself up, leaned over the bar, and snagged another shot glass. "What'll you give me?"

They both knew the only thing of value she had to offer was her body and the use of it, but not even his gorgeous, perfectly formed muscles would make her wager that. If she ever put her hands on Derek Ford, she wanted them both to know she was making a choice, not fulfilling an obligation.

So something else. Something that would make him smile. "Less backtalk. Or, you know, if you'd miss it...*more* backtalk."

He seemed to consider that. "A raise," he said finally. "So you can find a better place to live."

Her heart kicked again, harder this time. It made her chest squeeze so tight she couldn't draw a full breath. "That's what you want if you win?"

"Sure." He splashed whiskey into both glasses.

She could ask why he cared, but she already suspected the answer. *I don't,* he'd say, with some touch or smile that would flip her stomach inside out and make her wish she was just another girl, a normal one. Someone with innocence or experience, but not this painful, unnatural mixture of both.

"I know what I want if I win," she heard herself say, and the words that would have been so innocent a few moments ago felt suddenly suggestive—because they were. "A long, hot bath."

"Deal." He knocked back one shot and pushed the other over to her.

Remembering her ungraceful sputtering the first night, Mia braced herself. That had been only a tiny sip. This was more, burning down her throat like liquid flame. Heat bloomed in her chest and spiraled wider. Her cheeks grew warm. Her nipples felt tight, sensitive, though maybe that came from watching Ford.

His gaze flickered down to her chest. He turned away immediately to pour two more shots, but not before she saw the flash of fire in his eyes. "Drink up, buttercup."

She was going to lose. She could feel it already in the fuzzy anticipation as she lifted the second shot, in the way it didn't burn nearly as much on its way down. She was going to lose, and she should be ecstatic at the idea of higher pay and a new place to live.

Too bad she was stuck on the fantasy of sliding into a hot bath with him.

5

Little Miss Mia couldn't hold her liquor.

Ford laid a hand at the small of her back and winced as she swayed dangerously on the stairs. For a while, he'd thought he might have to carry her, and he'd been relieved when she managed to walk on her own. That relief would be shot to hell if she fell—and took him with her.

She straightened, and he breathed a sigh. "Steady, buttercup. You're almost there."

"I made a mistake." She gripped the railing and navigated the next steps with precise concentration. "I looked down. You can never look down. Or back."

"Words of wisdom." He had to slide his arm around her waist and urge her forward. "That's it. Nice and easy."

She shivered against him. "It was only three shots.

Why am I this warm?"

"Because alcohol makes your capillaries swell—" Good, maybe if he talked about blood vessels, it would distract him from the definite and inconvenient swelling going on below his belt. "It flushes your skin. Makes it heat up."

Only three more steps, but she managed to rub the sweet curves of her ass against him on every damn one of them. "You should have given me whiskey instead of a heater."

He gritted his teeth. "The warming effect is temporary. When it wears off, you'll be colder than ever." Cold, and passed out in his office.

Or his bed.

Ford shoved the thought away and led her to the couch along the wall adjacent to his desk. "Time to sleep it off, Mia."

"But it's not even lunchtime." She tumbled to the cushions, adorably disheveled, and stared up at him. "I can't sleep if you're going to give me a raise. I need to do something brilliant."

"You're welcome to get up and try, but I think you're better off staying put."

"Do you always get your way?"

A simple question, not a challenge. "Usually. I've learned to pick my battles, buttercup. I fight the ones I can win."

"That's smart." She closed her eyes and tilted her head back. "I didn't have a choice. I didn't think I'd win, but I had to fight."

A lock of hair fell across her face, and Ford brushed it away. "Shows what you know, then. You're here, aren't you?"

"I'm here." She turned into his touch, chasing it with her cheek. "I'm not miserable, you know. I don't care if I live in a closet with no hot water and no lights. I don't care if you growl and snarl and snap at me. It's magic. All of it's magic, because I'm *here*."

She really was beautiful—full lips, big eyes, and delicate bones under smooth, dark skin. And he'd been treating her like shit, taking out his frustrations and thwarted desires on her.

It would serve him right if she slapped him instead of looking up at him with dreams in her eyes.

But she didn't. She slid her fingers up his arm, tracing his muscles with a featherlight touch. "I don't know how to flirt when it's real. I don't know how to want. Wanting was never my role."

Goose bumps rose on his skin. "You don't want to flirt with me, Mia."

"Because you don't want a whore?"

She sounded so sad, resigned. "Because you don't want me," he corrected gently. "Old and busted, that's what I am."

"So? I'm young and busted. I was cynical about sex before anyone ever touched me." Her fingernails dug into his skin suddenly, her grip fierce. "And then no one ever did, because I was already dirty. He should have gotten a damn Rose. At least she would have known how to pretend."

Her patron. Ford knew jack shit about the man, and he hated him. "Go to sleep, sweetheart, before the room starts spinning and you get sick."

She clung to him a moment longer before her hand slipped away. "I should have bet a kiss, win or lose. That would have been clever. I'm supposed to be clever."

His jeans pinched as he rose, and Ford tried to hide his wince. By the time he took a step back, her eyes had drifted shut.

By the time he reached his desk, she was snoring softly, the way only a person who was passed-out drunk could.

Later, he would have to talk to her. He would have to hear what she had been trying to say and respond like a functional human being. But for now…

All he wanted to do was hide.

Mia had a brand-new jacket, a full stomach, and a fuzzy ache in her skull that meant she needed to stay the hell away from O'Kane liquor.

Especially since fuzzy heads talked too damn much.

Little wonder Ford had opted out of taking her shopping himself. After she'd slept off the worst of the booze, he'd shoved her out of his office with Trix as fast as he could, shutting the door behind her with a haste that felt like its own statement.

At least roaming the market with Trix had been educational. She'd worked for the O'Kanes for years before becoming a member, which meant she knew the sector. Not just the places where Ford could stride, cockily unaware of how his dick kept him as safe as his ink, but the best ways to get by when you had neither.

She'd even helped Mia find a new apartment only three blocks away from the O'Kane compound. One glance at Trix's wrists, and the landlord had "remembered" a room opening up at the end of the week, and for only a little more than Mia was paying now.

Ink talked in Sector Four. O'Kane ink *screamed*.

Knowing she'd be gone soon made it easy to shrug off the darkness in the stairwell of her own dingy apartment building. Mia dug into her pocket for her key as she reached the second floor, but paused on the landing.

Mrs. Jones's door was ajar, but no light spilled out of it. Footsteps scuffled just inside, and worry cinched tight in Mia's chest. The woman was mean as hell, but she was also old. It wouldn't take much of a fall to crack frail bones and leave her helpless.

Fisting a hand around her keys, Mia took a careful step forward. "Mrs. Jones?"

The door swung open, and she found herself with the cold barrel of a pistol pressed against her forehead. "You're nosy. Know what happens to nosy bitches?"

She'd known fear, but the unforgiving metal digging into her skin was a threat so unfamiliar she could only feel foolish in those first seconds. The terror she'd felt in Sector Two had been pale compared to this. A patron might be cruel to a girl. He might force himself on her, knowing no one would consider it rape when he'd paid for the privilege. Every day in Sector Two presented a thousand possible reasons to die on the inside.

But no one would have killed her. No one would have dared.

She tried to move her numb lips, tried to say *anything*, but a gloved hand came out of the darkness, closing around the wrist of the man holding the gun. "Not her. She was rolling with O'Kane's redhead earlier."

The thug hesitated, bared his teeth. "You sure?"

"Saw them in the market. Lay off, man."

After an interminable moment, the pistol clicked, and the man backed away. "Looks like your lucky day, sweet cheeks."

She didn't move. The man brushed by, jostling her with his shoulder. More followed, streaming past her in silence, some carrying bulky bags heavy with looted goods.

One crossed into the fading light from the window, and his features were familiar. She'd seen him in the market earlier, traveling with a half-dozen friends, only memorable because they'd been swaggering, tossing glares left and right and laughing as people scurried out of their way.

Until they saw Trix.

Trix hadn't swaggered. She'd barely acknowledged their presence, but that had been enough to deflate their bravado.

Apparently it was also enough to keep Mia alive.

One of the men laughed as they tramped down the stairs, leaving Mia counting their steps while her pulse throbbed in her ears. The slamming of the front door cracked through the night, but the sound broke her from frozen terror.

Shaking, she rushed for Mrs. Jones's open door. It was dark inside, the usual hum of the generator silenced, but the old woman was sprawled in the dim light near one of the windows. Limp. Motionless.

Then she groaned, and Mia almost tripped over herself rushing across the intervening space. "Mrs. Jones?"

The woman heaved a shuddering breath that turned into a cough, and blood splattered her already stained white shirt. "Go," she wheezed. "Run—"

"They're gone," Mia promised, tugging at the blood-soaked flannel shirt beneath her hands. Buttons pinged in all directions as she gave up and tore, but there wasn't enough light to see the wound, and there was so much blood. Warm, wet, and still pumping sluggishly from someplace beneath Mia's fingers.

"You'll be okay." They both knew it was a lie, but what else could she say? The only real comfort she could offer was the promise of vengeance—but maybe that worked in Sector Four. She found one of the old lady's hands and curled her own around it. "We'll find them. My boss will find them."

But she said nothing. No last words of hope, farewell, or even anger. She just went limp, her half-closed eyes devoid of life.

A loud bang echoed from down the hall, and Mia started, letting Mrs. Jones's hand slip from hers. She staggered to her feet and inched toward the door, and it was like walking through a dream. Nothing felt real. She pressed a hand to the doorframe to steady herself, but the bloody hand clutching at the faded wood was unfamiliar. Chipped nails, ragged cuticles, skin roughened and dry from cheap soap and a lack of the lotions and creams she'd never noticed until they were gone. It didn't look like the hand she'd had for most of her life, and she couldn't feel the wall beneath it.

She couldn't feel anything.

But she remembered this sensation. Cloudy, fuzzy, barely feeling the ground beneath her shoes, unable to hear anything past her pulse throbbing in her ears. She'd walked out of Vaughn's house like this, certain she'd be caught, dragged low, punished for thinking she deserved more, deserved *better*—

God, she had to get out of here. Get out and never come back, which meant finding the courage to move. She'd sleep under the bar if she had to, or plead with Ford to let her spend a few nights on the couch. He cared, under that grumpy façade. He didn't want to, but she didn't care. Pity was better than dying in a gutter.

She lifted her free hand to her throat. Her jacket was in the way, but she didn't have to tug down her zipper to know her locket wasn't there. She always left it behind, tucked away with her meager savings, afraid to wear something shiny and silver that might catch the attention of a desperate thief.

The money would be hard to pay back, but the locket—if they'd taken her locket—

Breathe. The scent of blood turned her stomach, but deep breaths got her out into the hallway. She scurried to her door, hope withering when she saw it standing open, splintered where the lock should have been.

Inside was chaos. Her table was shattered. Someone had taken a knife to her thin mattress, ripping it apart to look for valuables. The space heater Ford had sent her was gone, along with her solar recharger and lamp.

Her box lay on its side a few feet into the room, the lid torn away. Empty.

Wet warmth ran down her cheek. A tear, which she swiped away with a shaking hand. Nothing left was worth taking with her. Nothing left was worth saving—except for her life. And if she wanted to keep that, she didn't have time for tears.

So for the second time in a month, she choked them back, choked back terror, and put one foot in front of the other.

As long as she was breathing, that was all she could do.

Ford worked until his eyes were gritty, burning.

At first, he settled in with his charts and spreadsheets as a way to distract himself from thoughts of Mia. She was strong, he'd give her that. Stronger than he'd expected. Every time he threw a challenge her way, she met it not only with defiance but competence.

Well, except for the liquor, but he could hardly blame her for that.

The distraction served its purpose, keeping him

occupied long enough for his attention to morph into something else—the sincere and utter absorption in his work. This was where he belonged, building the O'Kanes' business, one deal at a time. Other men pounded the streets, keeping order and helping Dallas rule over the immediate, mundane concerns of a king.

Ford was building an empire.

He was damn good at it, and maybe—just maybe— he could teach Mia to do it, too. She was bright. It would only take—

Footsteps on the stairs drew his attention, and he was already rising from his chair when a shaky knock rattled his office door. He pulled it open, and his heart shot up into his throat.

Mia stood there, pale and covered with blood. "I'm sorry. I—I know it's late—"

He dragged her inside and slammed the door behind her. "Are you hurt? What the fuck happened?"

She looked down at her bloody hands and shuddered. "The old woman who owned my building. She's dead. They took everything."

"Shit." She was trembling, her skin chilled. She was slipping into shock, and he had to snap her out of it. "Mia, look at me."

She didn't. She barely seemed to hear him as she curled her fingers toward her palms. "I'm okay. One of them saw me with Trix, so they didn't shoot me."

Christ. "Did they touch you?" He resisted the urge to shake her—barely. "Is any of this blood yours?"

"No." She blinked and lifted her chin, her eyes focusing on his with effort. "Just here," she whispered, brushing a reddened spot on her forehead and leaving a streak of blood behind. "He pressed the—the gun—" She swallowed a choked noise. "I'm okay. I'm sorry, I'm okay."

"No, you're—" She wasn't hurt, but he wasn't helping her, either. "Sit." He swung her around and eased her down to the couch. "I'll just be a second."

He snatched up the tablet from his desk, activating it with a swipe of his thumb. He tapped the screen to open the communications program. For the first time, he cursed his wide, clumsy fingers as he attempted to compose an alert.

Trouble on South Side. Time to mobilize.

Quickly, he filled in the rest of the details, sent the message to Dallas, and threw down the tablet.

Mia was still sitting on the couch, her shoulders slumped, her entire body hunched in, as if she didn't want to take up too much space. She lifted her head, and at least there was sense in her eyes now. But there was something else, too, something too fragile to call hope.

She wet her lips and looked away. "They took the heater you gave me."

Like he gave two shits about that. "Dallas has a dozen more in storage," he told her as he lifted her from the couch and into his arms. "Don't worry about it."

He made his way into the bathroom with slow, careful steps. He dropped Mia to her feet, reached in to cut on the hot water, and began to undress her. She didn't resist as he stripped away her bloody jacket and pulled her sweater over her head.

The thin undershirt beneath it clung to her skin as steam filled the room, and she caught his wrists, her grip desperate. "You don't have to do this. I—I was just going to ask if I could sleep on your couch."

"Shh. You need to get cleaned up."

"Why?" Her voice broke, and tears gathered on her thick eyelashes faster than she could blink them away. "Why do you—?"

Care. She didn't say it, but the word hung between them anyway. His usual flippant response—*I don't*—would have been cruel, especially with a sobbing woman pressed against his chest.

The truth was, Ford did care, and that was what had him climbing into his shower fully clothed with a naked, blood-spattered woman.

He backed her under the shower spray and let the water sluice down over her head. "You'll be all right, Mia. Trust me."

Under the hot water and his gentle touches, her trembling finally eased. Her clothes had protected her from most of the blood, but it took time to work it out of her hair, and she buried her face against his throat as he did so, hiding her silent, heartbreaking tears.

"You'll stay here tonight," he told her softly. "I'll take the couch."

She turned her head, but didn't lift it to look at him. She pressed her cheek to his shoulder as the last pinkish water circled the drain and her body relaxed against his. "You don't have to."

There was no mistaking the yearning in her voice. Whether it stemmed from fear or the need for comfort, he didn't know, and it didn't matter. "Yes, I do. You take the bed, and you'll be square in the morning."

She didn't speak again until he'd cut off the water and found a towel to wrap around her. She clutched it against her breasts and finally met his gaze, and it was like the afternoon when he'd knocked the hope out of her, only worse. "It's not just tonight. I don't have anywhere to go until next week."

"We'll find you a room here, or you can bunk with one of the girls. Now stop thinking."

Clutching her towel tighter, she gave him a tiny, lopsided smile. "You meant it, didn't you? I'm going to be all right."

That smile rattled his defenses. "I don't lie, but-tercup. If I say it, it's truth."

She didn't answer at first, just stared at him with those gorgeous brown eyes, and he could see the strug-gle in her. The yearning that softened her gaze and the stubborn hope curving her lips. The lingering fear in her clenched fists and the shadows of pain in the stiff, wary set of her shoulders.

She looked tired. Beaten down but not defeated, because she was still smiling, still fighting. She wrin-kled her nose at him and stared down at the towel. "I don't have any clothes. That will be awkward for work tomorrow."

"We'll find you some. Now, what did I say?" He steered her out of the bathroom, but instead of taking a right down the hallway, back toward the office, he guided her to the left.

Into the bedroom.

He was the worst sort of asshole, bringing her here when he knew it would be impossible not to close his eyes and imagine her here under different circum-stances. Far less traumatic circumstances. But Ford had long ago learned to accept the fact that he was a dick, so he pushed her toward the bed and pulled back the covers.

She balked again, the towel sagging as she lifted a hand to the disheveled hair curling damply against her bare shoulders. "I'll get your pillow wet."

He couldn't tell her how many nights he'd trudged from the shower straight to bed, too exhausted and achy to do *anything* but collapse, even something as simple as drying his hair.

So he grunted and pulled the towel up to soak the worst of the water from her dark curls. "You're high-maintenance."

She made a choked noise, squeaky and high—laughter edged with hysteria, as if all the tension was bubbling out of her. "If you think this is bad, wait until I can afford to pamper myself."

"Can't wait, buttercup."

When the worst of the water was squeezed away, she slipped between the sheets, settling in with a soft sigh of pleasure. "I'm going to get spoiled again, and then you'll win all the arguments by offering me fancy sheets or soft pillows. I'm on to you, Derek Ford."

The white sheet clung to her wet skin in places, turning transparent as it molded to her curves. "I'm an O'Kane. We may not be showy, but we do like our luxuries."

She made an amused little noise and rolled onto her side, presenting him with the smooth line of her spine as the sheet molded to her waist and barely covered the flare of her hip. "As long as you don't expect me to be one of them. I disappointed my patron daily. Sometimes hourly."

The words distracted him from the sight of her stretched out in his bed. "You're not a luxury, for fuck's sake. You're a person."

"I know." She jerked the covers up to hide her body as she sprawled onto her back again. Wary this time, blinking up at him from bloodshot eyes with her hair in a damp tangle around her head. "But it's hard," she whispered, twisting the sheets around her trembling fingers. "It's hard to remember I have a right to be... imperfect. It's the first rule—never let a man see the real you."

"So I gather." The rules were different for men, but no less restrictive. Never let them see you weak—the reason Ford had been hiding away in his office. "But fuck 'em, right?"

She reached out and brushed her fingers across the back of his hand. "Do you have to go?"

He hesitated. Best to go before either of them started getting ideas about anything. "I can stay," he said finally. At least until she fell asleep.

She wiggled to the opposite side of the bed in silence, and Ford stared down at her for a moment before stripping his wet shirt over his head. It only made sense to undress. He was dripping all over the damn floor, making a mess, and what was he going to do anyway? Stand there beside the bed and gawk at her all night?

She turned her head as he reached for his belt, and he finished undressing in silence, torn between gratitude and the perverse desire to make her turn around and watch him.

He dragged on a clean, dry pair of underwear, turned off the lamp, and stretched out on top of the covers, careful to keep his distance. He lay there, rigid and still, listening to her breathing.

After an endless silence, she wiggled closer, invading his space like she'd been doing from the start. She didn't speak, didn't reach for him. Just pressed her forehead to his shoulder, her breath skating down his arm.

The soft caress raised goose bumps on his skin, and Ford sighed as Mia's breathing deepened and slowed. She'd been invading his space, all right, and the worst part was that he was starting to be okay with it.

6

The bed was so soft, Mia didn't want to wake up.

She curled her toes against the silkiest sheets she'd ever felt and turned her face into the pillow. It still smelled like Ford—like his soap and whiskey and something sharp and delicious that might have been cologne or aftershave or her imagination.

Probably her imagination. But it was nice here, floating in warmth, decadence. She could summon the feel of his strong shoulder beneath her cheek, the heat of his skin. Maybe he'd be hot like that all over. Hot and hard, protecting her from the danger and roughness of the world.

Protecting her from himself, too. She'd woken just enough to feel the loss of him when he'd rolled stiffly from the bed, but she hadn't protested. Knowing him, he would have stretched back out on the bed and resumed his vigil, refusing to relax or rest.

And if she'd thanked him, he would have grumbled about it.

The guilt of knowing he was sleeping on the couch with an injured leg finally drove her from her cocoon of blankets and pillows. His bedroom was sparse compared to the luxury of the bed, but she found a stack of clean clothes on top of the dresser and stole one of his T-shirts. It hung to mid-thigh and covered everything important, so she didn't bother with pants that wouldn't have fit her in any case.

Ford was still asleep in his office, squeezed awkwardly onto the couch. Guilt surged again, and she crept close enough to reach for the blanket that had slipped to his waist. A tattoo covered the left side of his chest—an old-fashioned motorcycle with a banner floating across the handlebars proclaiming his allegiance to the O'Kanes.

She pulled the covers up, and he shifted with a grunt, rolling onto his side before stiffening with another noise, this one far more like a groan.

He had to be in agony. She'd seen the stiffness caused by a few hours in his chair—what would a night on a too-small couch do to him? There were no rugs out here to soften the cool floor, but she'd knelt on equally unforgiving surfaces. She lowered herself beside the couch and laid a hand on his shoulder. "Ford? Why don't we switch places?"

He flinched away from her touch. "I'm fine," he growled.

His snarls would never scare her again, not after last night. "Of course you are," she replied, putting bite in the words. "But I'm not going to lounge around in your bed while you hurt your leg out of stubborn pride. So I'll just kneel here and shiver, and we can be miserable together."

He moved fast, dragging her off the floor as he sat up. She landed astride his lap—astride his *cock*, which was hard beneath the thin layers of fabric separating them—and he locked both hands around her waist. "Don't treat me like a child," he rasped. "I'm far from helpless, and don't you fucking forget it."

She couldn't drag in a full breath. His erection felt enormous. Unforgiving. Every soft, sleepy fantasy she'd ever had about him came roaring back, prickling over her skin and waking nerves gone numb from neglect.

But as good as he felt, she had to twist away. She recognized that soft ache, the heat building in her pussy. A few more wiggling rocks, and she'd be wet enough for him to feel it.

Embarrassment set her on fire as she braced both hands on his shoulders. "I never called you helpless. How can you even *think* that, when I'm the one who needs everything?"

"Because I see the way you look at me—like I'm some kind of harmless stray dog who only needs a little love." His hands glided up to close around her upper arms, and he jerked her down close to his face. "You don't even realize I could savage you with a bite."

Maybe he was right, and she should be scared. Not melting, shivering.

Wanting.

"You're wrong," she whispered, and she had to steal his breath from the tiny space between them. "I've known you could savage me from the start. I've been bitten. I'm still bleeding."

He arched up, grinding his hips against hers, and a tiny shudder wracked him. "You're getting wet."

The strained approval beneath the words killed her self-consciousness. She gasped as his next rock put pressure on her clit, and it was hard to focus now, to frame his face and force him to look at her.

"You're not harmless," she said softly, willing him to believe her. "I didn't run to a stray, toothless mutt for protection. I ran to the snarly beast who grumbles and tolerates me, because I still believe you'd tear out the throat of anyone who came after me."

He didn't answer, just ran his right hand up the inside of her thigh. His skin burned, just as she'd known it would, but she hadn't been prepared for the rasp of his work-roughened fingers, so different from her own.

Already dizzy from anticipation, she dropped her hands to the solid muscles of his shoulders and lifted her hips in quiet, shameless invitation. Finally, someone would touch her. Someone would *want* her.

His hand reached the top of her thigh, curling beneath her, brushing the curve of her ass and almost— *almost*—all the places she ached.

Then he stopped.

Shuddering, she dug her nails into his shoulders and tried to shift into his touch. But he held her like that, starving, needing, everything inside her twisted tight and ready. It was agonizing, it was torture—and it was making her wetter.

The trainers had pithy words about this, too. About games of power, and how they could exhilarate both parties.

Except Mia wasn't playing. She was trembling. "Ford—*Derek*. Please. Please—"

He leaned in and slowly drew his tongue over the ridge of her collarbone, from her shoulder to the center of her chest.

Oh, God.

Her nipples tightened to aching points, and getting naked suddenly seemed like the most important thing in the world. She tangled her fingers in her stolen shirt, but Ford stopped her with a muttered warning. "Uh-uh. Don't move."

She froze.

His growl melted into an approving hum, and he used his free hand to guide the worn cotton over her head. It fell to the floor, and she struggled for equilibrium as Ford's gaze raked over her, hot and intense.

He was nothing like Vaughn. He was the opposite—rough where Vaughn had been civilized, raw in all the ways Vaughn had been polished. But for a terrible moment those differences didn't matter, because Vaughn had stared at her with intensity, too. Intensity laced with hunger, and so much self-loathing he couldn't shoulder the burden.

So he'd heaped it on her shoulders, instead.

She'd escaped from Sector Two, but the weight of it still pressed down on her as Ford's gaze swept back over her breasts and toward her face. "What do you see?" she whispered, barely daring to hope.

"Soft." His breath caressed her skin. "Sweet." He licked her again, tracing his tongue down the curve of one breast. "Beautiful." He sucked her nipple into his mouth with a groan.

It was too much. She gasped and sank her fingers into his short hair, clutching at the back of his head as her own tipped back. Sharp, bright points of pleasure flared every time he sucked, and there was nothing lazy or easy about it.

She opened her mouth—to ask, plead, *something*—and his hand shifted, his fingers slipping through wet folds. He found her clit with a firm, circling touch that never seemed to cease, only recede and come rushing back as each rough fingertip slid over her in turn.

"Oh—" It was all she could say, the same noise

over and over again. She was gasping, panting, squirming on his fingers without grace or thought or any care to how awkward it would be the next time she had to sit down at his desk and try to concentrate on work and not how it felt to be riding his hand.

He wound a hand in her hair and tugged her head back. "Do it again."

She wasn't doing anything, and that realization should have terrified her. There was no thought in her now, no control. Every sound, every movement—it was pure impulse. Instinct and desire.

Truth.

The reckless danger of it only made everything hotter. He'd bared her throat, his fingers twisting tight enough in her hair to trip the line between pleasure and pain, and his words drifted back, a memory edged with new heat.

I could savage you with a bite.

She lifted her chin higher with a shaky moan, offering him the vulnerable line of her throat in silent trust.

He took it, closing his teeth on her skin with a groan. His fingers pushed deeper, curling into her as he pressed the heel of his palm against her clit.

Her body seized. The bite was delicious pain, the kind that burned into pleasure, but his fingers— She'd known it would sting, but his fingers were so broad and there were *three* of them, and she was so far past deception. She couldn't bite back her hiss of pain or hide her flinch as she struggled to relax, to adjust—

It was his turn to freeze.

She took a careful breath and squeezed her eyes shut. "I'm sorry. I just—I need a second—"

"Shh." He didn't stop, only eased back until the blunt tip of one finger remained inside her. "Like this."

The discomfort had already faded. One finger was enough to stretch gently as she rocked onto it, pushing him deeper, and she shuddered as that need built, slower this time. Fuller, somehow, and not only because she was hyperaware of the intimacy of taking him into her body.

Another finger joined that one as Ford licked the bitten spot on her neck and made another low noise. "That's it, baby. Take it."

Approving words, and God, she hadn't realized how badly she needed it. Discomfort didn't matter. She clutched at his hair and panted, willing her body to relax, to accept him, to welcome the way he stroked deep and filled her. "I'll take more," she whispered shakily. Begged. "Let me, for you."

"Damn straight you will," he growled. "When I give it to you. Say it, Mia."

She lifted her head and met his eyes, and even though the world felt hazy, he was sharp. All perfect lines, strong jaw, and full lips. His brows lowered over intense, commanding eyes, and her heart pounded.

Her choice. This wasn't Sector Two, and no man would ever own her again. It was her choice, and she'd already made it when she bared her throat to him. "Yes. I'll take what you give to me."

"When I give it to you."

The pressure inside her was shifting toward discomfort again, but not from the size of his fingers. She wanted to rock and squirm against the heel of his hand until the achy tension snapped. It was torture to hold still like this, shaky and helpless as she stared at a release she couldn't quite reach.

But that was the game, wasn't it? Granting him power, trusting in the implicit promise that he'd give her something in return. That was the lie everything in Two was built on—the promise no man was expected to keep.

She wasn't in Sector Two anymore.

Mia dropped her hands to his broad shoulders and splayed her fingers wide, struggling with the temptation to simply move and seek her own pleasure. "I'll take what you give me," she repeated softly, her voice only trembling a little. "When you give it to me."

"*Yes.*" His fingers curled inside her, and he rotated his hand against her clit in slow circles of pressure, each one harder than the last, each one sparking along her nerves until she was on fire. "And I will, baby. I'll fucking give it to you."

"Oh—" she gasped, and that was all she got out before she flew apart.

Her body clenched. All of it, but nothing as fast and hard as her pussy, and even the throbbing pleasure couldn't wipe away awareness of how exposed she was. He'd feel every shuddering pulse as she squeezed tight around his fingers, the proof that she wanted him.

Wanted *more.*

He continued to stroke her, slowing bit by bit, until she could think again. Then he pulled his hand away and settled it on her hip. "You've got a story, don't you, Mia?"

Her limbs were liquid. She dropped her head to his shoulder, huddling close to all that warm skin. "Everyone has a story these days."

"But yours is particularly interesting, I can tell."

She wanted to play dumb, but it would have been another lie. A rebellious one, perhaps, but still deception. So she was blunt, instead. Crude. "Not really. Virgin whores are Sector Two's most valuable commodity. Because that's all that counts, right? Not what I know, not what I've done. Just whether or not some guy gets to be the first to shove his dick into me."

"I guess," he agreed quietly. "I don't know a whole hell of a lot about Two."

He hadn't reacted with anger or distaste, and some of the tension eased from the knot that had formed between her shoulder blades. Turning her cheek to his chest, she lifted her other hand to trace his collarbone, and the fact that he allowed the idle caress relaxed her further.

She was safe here. As safe as anyone could be, and that made it easier to talk. "They handle most of Eden's trade with other cities. That's why it's so nice there compared to the other sectors, and why we had so many extravagant things. We—they got the luxury in exchange for taking all the risks."

"And why all their customs look so pretty—on the outside."

Yes, Ford would understand the business advantages. "Orchids have the most intense training, but the girls are meant to be more than companionship. We're hostesses. Entertainment. Assets."

She hesitated, her fingertip poised at the base of his throat. He had stubble, a lot of it, and now she knew how it felt against her skin. The intoxicating rasp of it, the shivery sensation. He was still hard beneath her, and if she shifted just right, the ridge of his cock would grind tauntingly against her sensitive pussy.

Might as well tell him all of it. A man like Ford must already suspect, if he didn't know outright. "And we're...spies, I suppose. I had a patron, but my loyalty was never meant for him. I learned that before I knew anything else."

Ford snorted. "No shit. It wouldn't do Cerys any damn good to train up her girls and then let them go, not really."

"Because you're thinking about her like she's a businessperson." It was amazing how many men in Two didn't, even though Cerys ruled the sector as surely as Dallas O'Kane held Sector Four. "They don't think it's odd that she'd spend years training women to sell to them. Because the men think they deserve us. That they're entitled to us."

"Then what they really deserve is to get their dumb asses spied on." Ford tilted her head up with his finger under her chin. "Who was he? The man who thought he was entitled to you?"

"Vaughn Tyler." Even the name tasted bitter, but she managed a wry smile. "It's funny, in a way. He didn't think virginity had anything to do with his dick, either. I wasn't vapid and ignorant, so that meant I was filthy and used up before he ever touched me. Which is why he didn't."

"You know that's bullshit, right?"

"Yes," she snapped. "If I believed it, I'd still be there, letting him—" She ground her teeth together and jerked her gaze from his before her vulnerable defensiveness showed him everything. "I'm sorry. I know it's bullshit. I *do*. But it was getting under my skin. Anything will, if you give it long enough."

Ford nodded slowly. "Yeah, it will. Sometimes in ways you don't even realize."

It was true, and Ford was proof of it. It was like she was riddled with thorns that had been there so long she couldn't feel them anymore, not until Ford brushed a sensitive spot and pulled one free. First the sting, then the giddy relief—

But it went both ways. He'd ground a few deeper, too, and would do it again if she kept hiding the things that hurt her. And one thorn was buried so deep, the thought of being free of it left her dizzy.

She wiggled back, careful not to put too much weight on his legs as she lifted her body from his and curled her fingers under the waistband of his underwear.

He locked his fingers around her wrist. "I wasn't just waiting out my turn to get off."

"I know," she whispered, meeting his eyes. "I want—" Words failed her. She wanted something selfish, something impossible to explain without laying out the ugly truth and killing the moment. She'd have to tell him about those miserable trips to Vaughn's office. The heavy smell of liquor. The shadows, everywhere except for the sad bit of carpet where she knelt, naked but for her pride.

Neither of them had enjoyed those nights. Oh, Vaughn had achieved physical release every time, his fist sliding over his cock, fast and furtive, his gaze jumping across her body with hunger and loathing. But he'd hated it. He'd blamed her for every agonizing second, from the first stirrings of his unwanted erection to the instant he spilled across his hand, furious at his own weakness.

So he'd vented it on her. *Slut* and *whore* and *filthy temptress* and a hundred boring variations that she'd done her best to tune out, letting them roll past her like meaningless sound. That was all they'd ever been—a pitiful man's guilt and confusion, all because blaming her was easier than accepting himself.

They'd still gotten under her skin.

None of that was in Ford's eyes now as he watched her, or in his voice as he let go of her wrist. "Okay. Just wanted you to know, that's all."

Her hands shaking, she freed his erection. It was every bit as large as she'd imagined, hot and hard beneath her touch. And thick—her thumb didn't meet her fingertips when she circled the shaft, and she shivered at the thought of rising up on her knees and trying to take him into her body. It would take patience to do it without pain—or a need that transcended discomfort.

She had a different need right now, one that left no room for patience as he wrapped his hand around his cock.

"The night I met you," she whispered, "you offered to jerk off in front of me."

"I remember." He stroked the hard length once—and grinned.

All those lazy, sated places inside her tensed with renewed interest, and she swore she could taste her own racing pulse as she watched his hand. "Does looking at me make you hard?"

"Every time you lick your lips, buttercup."

And he'd never hate her for it. She proved it by letting her tongue dart out, swiping it across her lower lip. "You like my tongue?"

"Mmm." He followed her movements, then pressed his thumb between her lips. "I do."

She caught his thumb between her teeth and licked the tip. Slow, taunting, the way she'd lick his cock if he asked her nicely enough, warm and wet and easy until he got growly and demanded more.

"I can jerk myself off," he said casually. Lazily. "Or you could show me what else you can do with your tongue."

Oh, she could do so many things. Dirty things, clever ones—things she'd never had the opportunity to try on someone whose dark eyes sparked with such intense hunger that no attempts to be casual could cover it.

She'd seen boredom. There were men in Orchid House—handsome, vacant men who could be trusted not to cross any lines or develop affections. They endured clumsy blowjobs with relaxed stoicism, offering bland critiques and even blander encouragement, everything carefully sterile and technical.

Uninspiring.

Ford was anything but. She let his thumb slip free of her lips and turned to nuzzle his hand, dizzy with anticipation and something else, something wild. The game that they'd started playing and hadn't quite stopped, with its slippery exchange of power and trust.

Trust was fragile to start. He could have ordered her to her knees, demanded she part her lips. He could have fucked her mouth so deep she choked on his dick. She would have obeyed because she wanted to, but some tiny part of her would have wondered if she'd done it because obedience was easy when it only scratched the surface.

This would be different. Deeper. She pressed her cheek to his palm and met his eyes, knowing he might never understand the significance of this moment, and how much it cost her to let go of the control that had kept her safe when it was the closest thing to freedom she'd ever tasted.

"You know the answer," she said, letting the words drop to a husky whisper that matched the heavy warmth uncurling inside her. "I'll take what you give me, when you give it to me."

Heat gleamed in his eyes. "That's right, Mia."

It was too much again, too intense. She broke free of his gaze and turned to kiss his fingertips, wishing desperately he'd already growled an order at her. Frantic and uncivilized—that felt good. She could drown in the passion instead of trembling through moments like this, naked and vulnerable, too aware she was being reckless with her body and her heart.

But when he spoke, it twisted her trembling even higher. "Go on, sweetheart," he growled, low and taunting. Tempting. "Suck my dick."

Yes.

No wonder Lex had come here, to these people who seemed oblivious to the idea of shame. Or maybe she'd helped corrupt them. Mia peeked at Ford's face as she slid to the floor, and his anticipation and approval mirrored everything inside her.

She couldn't shock him. Not by needing or wanting, not by being willing to take—or give. She stroked her fingers over his thighs. Fresh scars broke the skin of one leg, angry and jagged, and guilt twinged at the thought of him twisted onto this couch all night, suffering to give her space.

That wouldn't happen again. She made the silent promise to herself as one hand found his wrist. She traced her fingertip up to where he still held his shaft in a loose grip, teasing over his fingers before brushing her knuckle up the underside. "Have you imagined this moment?"

"You, on your knees? Your mouth?" The corner of Ford's mouth kicked up. "You bet your sweet ass."

Her hair had dried in tangled curls. They tumbled around her cheeks as she lowered her lips to caress the head, blocking her view of him. Not that she needed it—his body was alive with clues. The tension in his muscles, the hitch in his breathing when she darted her tongue out to tease.

His cock jumped in her hand. "Open up, Mia."

A choice that was no choice at all. Shivering, she parted her lips as wide as she could.

He guided her head down with a gentle touch. "Show me."

Closing her eyes, she let herself go and fell into

him. The spicy scent of him and the way he tasted on her tongue. And he was every bit as big as he'd seemed. She stopped when he reached the back of her throat, pausing only long enough to see if he'd push her deeper.

He didn't. His hand rested on her head, a warm and encouraging weight, but he let her set the pace—for now. Slow. Slow and wet, sliding up and down, savoring the chance to give pleasure for the joy of it.

He gathered her hair away with his other hand, clearing a view of her face, and his hips flexed as he rocked up into her mouth. "Pretty. So pretty."

Still soft. Easy. She drew up a little, curling her hand around his slick shaft to stroke as she focused everything she knew on breaking down his easy control. She needed him panting, desperate, his fingers snagging in her hair as he thrust up into her mouth. She needed him to *need* with the same helplessness he'd sparked in her.

He closed his hand around hers and squeezed tight. "Don't think. Just take."

Don't think.

It should have been dangerous. Oral sex was a skill, imparted to her with the same rules and guidelines as her lessons in tech and first aid. You analyzed responses, adjusted strategies, kept your control while stripping away his.

You didn't tremble. You didn't let yourself get swept away in the moment. And you *never* admitted the truth.

Lifting her head to stare up at him, Mia broke all the rules. "I'm nervous. It's never been real before."

But Ford only nodded, despite the heat blazing in his eyes. "So stop wondering how to get me off...and get me off."

Don't think. Take.

Without breaking eye contact, she lowered her head. Licked. Around the crown and up to the tip, where she found her proof that he was plenty aroused. Just a few drops of liquid, but she painted her lips with the taste of him before opening wide and taking him deep.

He bumped the back of her throat before her lips reached their fingers, but she didn't let that stop her this time. A shift in position, a tilt of her neck and she pushed again, her head swimming.

He groaned, holding her there for an endless heartbeat before dragging her up by her hair until only the head of his cock remained in her mouth. Back and forth, up and down, until he was shaking.

But still he held back, gritting out words through clenched teeth. "Show me how you want it, Mia. How do you want me to come?"

A dozen possibilities flashed through her mind. On her face. On her breasts. Spilling across her tongue. So many symbols, and the meaning and implications slipped away in a haze of drunken want.

She didn't care about where or how, just about *now*. She pulled their joined hands away and moaned, fighting his grip on her hair to take him deep, to take all of him. Ford ground out a curse and stiffened beneath her, his cock throbbing on her tongue as she swallowed him.

She stroked his hips until the tension went out of him, but when she lifted her head, her gaze refused to travel higher than his chest. Nervousness fluttered back to life as she fought to steady her breathing. As long as she stared at his chest, she was safe. If she looked into his eyes and saw disappointment, or disapproval—

—oh God, or worse, if she *didn't*—

He lifted his thumb to her mouth and rubbed it

over her lower lip. "What did they take?" he asked hoarsely. "From your apartment."

Surprise drew her gaze upward before she could stop it, and then it was all over. Relaxed pleasure or even approval would have been bad enough. Her heart was so starved for affection that the thought of mere tolerance made her giddy.

But that wasn't tolerance in his eyes. It was warmth, real affection. His whole face had softened, and he was smiling at her as he brushed his thumb back and forth in a caress she felt in her toes.

"Mia."

She tried to focus. "The money Jade gave me. The heater. My solar charger." Her heart lurched, pain tightening her chest. "And my locket. It wasn't worth much, I don't even think it was real silver. But it was special."

"A gift?" he asked quietly.

"A memento," she agreed. "From someone who's gone."

"I see." He tapped her shoulder and urged her up. "Come on. You can take a shower, and I'll find you some clothes."

Her hair swung around her shoulders, and a tiny shred of vanity resurfaced as she raised a hand to the tangled mess. "And a comb?"

"We'll get one of the girls to do your hair." He handed her the T-shirt she'd taken from his room. "It'll be okay, Mia. I promise."

He'd said those words before, but this time she believed him. It could have been the warmth lingering in his eyes or the matching heat in her body, or maybe she was just reckless. Throwing herself over the edge of a cliff because the fall was so, so exhilarating.

She rocked up on her toes and brushed a kiss to

his cheek. "I know. Are you going to shower with me?"

"Next time," he rumbled. "Gotta check in with Dallas."

Something new stirred, something a lot darker than vanity. There was nothing civilized about this feeling. Nothing tame. It was like a part of her she'd never realized was there had woken for the first time. It circled the memory of her landlady's limp, lifeless body and demanded blood.

Dallas O'Kane wouldn't have his current reputation if he wasn't willing to paint the walls with anyone who opposed him. That was probably what Ford was about to do—help Dallas track down and destroy the men who'd violated their sector.

The thought brought her savage, vicious pleasure. Maybe she belonged in Sector Four after all.

7

When he was pissed off, Dallas O'Kane moved fast.

"This is the one who held the gun to your girl's head," he told Ford as they surveyed the man chained to a chair.

The warehouse where they held their weekly cage fights was always dark around the edges, but Dallas had slapped the man down in the center, under the unforgiving glare of the largest, brightest light. "His friends gave him up fast enough," Dallas continued, crossing his arms over his chest with a dismissive snort. "They swore up and down that he was the only one who fucked with one of our people."

"Doesn't make the old lady any less dead." But Ford had no doubt Dallas had dealt with the others—quickly and with deadly force.

Which was good, because he had his own matters to attend to.

The punk in the chair squirmed under Ford's blank stare. He didn't look long on brains, but he had ears, and a mouth he seemed determined to run. "I didn't kill the old bitch."

"Do I look like the kind of man who gives a shit who pulled the trigger or held the blade?" Ford asked, taking one step closer. "You're judged by the company you keep, son."

"But I didn't—"

Dallas scoffed again, the derisive noise cutting enough to silence the protest. "You think he wants to hear excuses? Some of that shit you stole was his, so I'd get real quiet and real agreeable."

The kid didn't have a chance in hell of listening, but Ford spoke anyway. "You took some things that didn't belong to you. Now, I'm a fair bastard, really. Normally, I get it. People steal. Sometimes it's the only way to survive out here in the sectors. But a lot of things went down here that I don't fucking like."

That got him a stubborn, rebellious scowl. "We couldn't have known the girl was yours. She ain't got ink."

His. Instead of squashing the possessive satisfaction that roared up, Ford embraced it. "Someone knew well enough to stop you, someone who'd seen her with one of us. Now, what that says to me is you didn't do your due diligence. You know what that means, right?"

Angry silence.

Dallas endured it for five seconds before kicking the man's boot. "Answer his fucking question, or I'm gonna unchain you and let him at you."

The kid's gaze flicked from Dallas to Ford before he spit out a sullen, "No."

"It means doing your homework. Thinking before you act. Making damn sure that what you're about to do can't come back on you and your boys." Ford knelt in front of the chair. The kid couldn't have been more than twenty, still wet behind the ears. "Due diligence, that's lesson number one. You picking up what I'm laying down?"

He looked away. "Yeah. Yeah, fuck, I get it."

"Good. Where's the stuff?"

The kid shot another wary look at Dallas, who was doing his best impression of a bored king. He played it well, in part thanks to his ability to dominate a room from sheer presence alone. He didn't have to scowl to look intimidating, which made the moments when his lip kicked up in wry amusement all the more terrifying.

"You're looking for mercy from the wrong man," he drawled, lifting one hand to scratch his chin. "You think I want to be wasting my time with some sorry-ass wannabe so sad he has to roll great-grandma? Your only chance of walking out of here is making Ford real happy."

Ford knew Dallas wasn't likely to kill the kid—not for stealing—but whoever had pulled the trigger on the old lady had undoubtedly ended up good and dead. Judging from the thief's pallor, he'd seen it go down and believed he might be next.

"It's already sold," he said quickly, straining forward in the chains in his sudden rush to play nice. "All except the heater. I only have my share of the cash."

Ford snorted. "Of course it is. Where'd you unload the jewelry?"

"That wheezy fucker who just built the new place on the edge of town."

"Walt, huh?"

"Yes!" He twisted, lifting one hip. "The cash is in

my pocket. Take it, give it to the girl. I swear I won't get near her again."

"Well, I don't want the cash." Ford caught the kid by the chin in a hard grip. "I want the locket, and you and me are gonna go get it."

For a second, he looked well and truly baffled. "That piece of shit? Old man hardly gave us squat for it."

Oh, Ford deserved some kind of fucking medal for maintaining his composure. "Just because you couldn't fence it for a week's worth of booze and tits doesn't make it shit. It *means* something to my girl."

Brown eyes bulged in a pale face. The boy tried to nod, but Ford tightened his grip until he yelped. "Okay, okay! We'll get the piece. And then we're square?"

"Not even close, son. I'm also gonna beat your ass—*then* we'll be square."

"What?" He twisted harder, managing to yank his face away to shoot an entreating look at Dallas. "I told him what he wanted to know."

"So you did," Dallas agreed easily. "And after he kicks your ass, you'll be walking out of here. But if you don't like O'Kane justice, I'm happy to put you in the river with your friend. Why don't you think it over while Ford and I have a chat?"

The kid blustered, but Ford ignored him as he and Dallas climbed out of the cage. "You think he can learn from his mistakes, O'Kane?"

Dallas didn't reply until they hit the edge of the room and pushed through to one of the old storage rooms. It was littered with random shit—every room in the complex was, because Dallas never threw away a damn thing—including a collection of extra booths they'd hauled out of the Broken Circle when they extended the stage.

"Fuck if I know," Dallas said, dropping to one. He sprawled his legs out in front of him and raised one eyebrow. "I'd say ten minutes of thinking about ending up as fish food should put him in a learning mood."

"If anything will," Ford agreed, dragging a cigarette out of his shirt pocket. "At least they went to Walt. He'll give us the locket, no questions asked."

Dallas huffed out a laugh. "Yeah, he will. Old bastard's got a soft spot for Lex."

"Of course, I'm still gonna drag this bastard out there and make him explain the situation."

"Good. If he's stupid enough to try to sell stolen goods to Walt again, we'll hear about it." Dallas tugged his own cigarette case free and studied Ford for a moment. "So. Your girl, huh?"

A look that piercing could make a man fidget, if he let it. "It scared the piss out of him, right?"

"Sure. That's why I used it." Dallas flicked open his lighter and raised an eyebrow. "Lot of fuss for a locket, though."

Maybe so, but there wasn't a single person in the sectors who hadn't lost something irreplaceable, something precious. Ford was tired of seeing it—or of looking the other way and telling himself it wasn't his problem.

And this was *Mia*.

"She might have wound up dead," he reminded Dallas. "Would have, if she hadn't gone shopping and been seen with Trix. Only random fucking chance kept her alive."

"Yeah." Dallas lit his smoke before snapping the lighter shut with a heavy sigh. "A lot has changed since you joined up, Ford, and you haven't been around much to see it. I've let you roam wild because you do good work and I trust you, but I need to know you, too. And you need to know me."

"That's fair." Dallas had given him plenty of freedom to make his own way, but the O'Kanes were only strong if they could stand together.

Dallas shook his head. "It's necessity. It was one thing when it was just Sector Four, and our biggest threat came from stomping out upstarts. But now we're spread thin trying to clean up Three, and shit's falling through the cracks. I don't care if she's barely been here a week—Mia's ours, and that's always meant something. Add that to the bootleggers..."

The little pissants who thought they could trade on Dallas O'Kane's legend and reputation to market their own liquor were as good as dead, but no matter. The fact that they'd managed to sell their cheap swill, packaged in fake O'Kane labels, at all was a blow to the gang.

Dallas's next steps were fraught, vital. He may as well have been tap-dancing on landmines. One wrong move could compromise his gang, his sector. His way of life.

Ford crushed out his cigarette. "So what do we do?"

"We recruit. We circle the wagons." Dallas exhaled smoke toward the ceiling before pinning Ford with a look. "No more loners, Derek. You're part of this. An O'Kane. And it kills me to know you hurt yourself worse crawling back here because you didn't think we'd come for you."

That made it sound so awful, as if he had no confidence in his brothers. "I didn't, okay? That's not why I started back after my accident. It was about *doing* something instead of just lying there, waiting."

"And I get that. But I need you to know, man. We would have found you. You don't have to spend your spare nights rolling through the latest orgy for that to be true."

Ford snorted. The sex was an undeniable perk—for some—but it was far from the only thing that bound the O'Kanes together. "Yes, sir."

Dallas rolled to his feet. "Good. And watch yourself with that girl. Lex wouldn't have thrown her at you if she couldn't handle your foul-ass mouth and pissy attitude, but women from Two will fool you. Especially Cerys's girls."

"Fool you how?"

His leader hesitated, staring at the ash on the end of his cigarette before dropping it to the ground and slamming his boot onto it. "When they're pissed, you'll know. Fucking hell, you'll know. But when they're hurt, or scared—" He shook his head. "By the time they let you see, sometimes it's too late."

His personal experience with Lex, no doubt, and Ford softened his next words by clapping his hand on Dallas's shoulder. "I'm not you, buddy. And she's not Lex. But I appreciate the advice, all the same."

"No, you don't. No one ever does." Dallas grinned and jerked his head toward the door. "Go rub the puppy's face in his own piss and see if he can learn. I've got to go play barbarian king."

"Uh-huh."

Ford pushed out into the main room. The kid had managed to scoot his chair nearly out of the harsh circle of light in the center of the ring, but it didn't matter. He'd be out of it soon enough.

The cage door clanged loudly as Ford hauled it open. "Moment of truth, son. You ready to go?"

His eyes rolled briefly toward the distant exit, as if he was trying to tell himself *go* meant *leave*, but snapped back to Ford as he climbed into the cage, hiding a wince as one awkward moment put too much weight on his bad leg.

He didn't hide it well enough. Shrewdness entered the boy's gaze as it dropped to Ford's healing leg. "I'm supposed to fight you?"

"You are." He loosened the chains and dragged them free with a clatter. "Don't get too cocky, kid. I was grinding punks like you into the dirt when you were still shitting your pants."

His opponent was on his feet in an instant, shaking blood into his arms as he circled to the side. "Yeah, when was that? Fifty years ago?"

"Close, smartass." Ford watched him. "Go on, get the feeling back in your arms. You'll need it."

The kid kept moving, even more confident now—which meant he was dumb as a goddamn rock, after all. Even if he'd had a chance of smacking Ford down, he didn't have a chance in hell of making it off the compound, much less beyond Dallas's reach. Any cunning he had was immediate, animal instinct without a thought to what came next.

His attack wasn't subtle. Hell, it was downright predictable. He darted in from too far away, not even bothering to feint. He drove his foot straight toward Ford's injured leg like it was the brightest idea anyone had ever come up with, and it was almost a shame to take him down.

Almost. Anyone who would go for a weak spot that quickly, that easily, was a bully, plain and simple. Ford caught him by the foot and hauled him off his feet, letting him fall to the concrete flat on his back.

The kid wheezed, rolling back and forth as he tried to catch the breath the fall had driven from his lungs. Ford knelt over him and grabbed him by the hair. "I've been nice so far. That can change real easy."

"Fuck—fuck *you*—" Thin and breathless, but he

spat at Ford and swung wildly, crashing both fists into the arm holding him.

"This? This is nothing." Ford pulled his semiautomatic pistol from the small of his back and pressed the end of the barrel hard against the kid's forehead. "Is this what you did? You like how it feels?"

He froze. The blackness of his pupils seemed to swallow his irises, but staring death in the face didn't make him humble. It made him defiant. "If you were a real man, you wouldn't have stashed your piece of ass in a dump on the edge of the sector. You're the one who put her in the wrong place at the wrong time."

"There you go again, with your shitty assumptions." Mouthing off, because he already thought he was dead. Even with his rage leashed, Ford had no desire to correct the kid's mistaken fatalism.

He bit out another curse, another insult, probably, something slurred and incomprehensible as he struggled so hard to twist away that he almost left a clump of his hair in Ford's fist. When he couldn't get away, he spat again. "Just fucking shoot me already. I knew you couldn't fucking fight fair."

"Hosing your brains out of the cage before the next fight night? Nothing would make me happier." Ford put the pistol away and leaned back. "But O'Kane doesn't operate that way. Make sure you thank him for my restraint, because he's the only goddamn reason you're walking out of here instead of hitching a ride in a garbage bag."

The boy almost pissed himself as he rolled away, shaking from adrenaline and relief. After a moment on his hands and knees, panting, he lifted his head to stare at Ford. "Does that mean I can go?"

He snorted. "Hell, no. But you can accompany me out to Walt's place, show me Dallas made the right call."

Obviously not what he'd wanted to hear, but Ford had to admit the kid faked it as he staggered to his feet and tried to pull his tough-guy demeanor back around him. "Sure, whatever."

"Uh-huh, *whatever*." Maybe the kid could learn. Maybe, eventually, he'd even figure out that Dallas had saved him from more than death.

Dallas had saved him from becoming part of the problem.

Mia couldn't imagine meeting Lex and not feeling awed, but it was a hundred times more intimidating to face her like this.

Presentation was everything, and the woman who ruled Sector Four at Dallas O'Kane's side knew that. She was flawless. Not in the ways an outsider might notice, but in all the ways that mattered, the ones that sent a silent message about who she was.

What she was.

It started and ended with the tattoos. Ink wrapped her wrists, the O'Kane emblem framed by a pattern of delicate, beautiful lace. Except when you got close enough, the lace was made from delicate strands of barbed wire, sharp and deadly, as if someone had distilled what an Orchid should be into a single, compelling image.

There were more. Dallas's name swooping just below her belly button, so casually visible Mia knew the corset and jeans had been designed to frame it. The mark around her throat was the same, a crowned skull in colors so vivid, no one would ever forget who they were dealing with.

No, Lex was perfect from the top of her upswept

hair to the chunky heels of her expensive leather boots, and Mia was painfully aware of the messages her own appearance sent. Tangled hair that hadn't seen a stylist or a bottle of conditioner in a month, chipped nails and unmoisturized skin—

And Ford's clothes. His shirt, hanging to her knees, and she could protest all day long that she'd pulled it on out of necessity. It wouldn't change the possessive message, and Lex wouldn't miss it, even if she chose to ignore it.

"Primped, polished, and waxed, and all without lifting a finger," Lex murmured, raising one eyebrow. "That's damn near the only thing I ever missed about Sector Two."

Mia managed a shaky smile. "I wouldn't mind a visit to the spa. The hot pools, especially."

"I bet, honey." She held up the folded stack of clothing in her hands. "Ford said you needed a change of clothes. One. Because he's a man, I guess, and they'd all live in the same T-shirt and jeans forever if they could get away with it."

From what she'd seen of his wardrobe, Ford practically did. Oh, he might change the actual item, but the T-shirt she was wearing had a twin tossed over a chair and another couple folded up amidst his clean laundry. She reached for the clothes with a relieved smile. "I appreciate it. I feel like I'm forever saying thank you to O'Kanes, and it's not enough. But thank you."

"We'll get you more stuff, first thing." She tilted her head. "Well, almost first thing. We need to do your hair."

"The trainers would be horrified," Mia agreed, lifting a hand to the rough strands. "Blow-drying it straight hasn't exactly been my top priority." Or possible.

"Why would you?" Lex stepped up and pulled her

hand away from her hair. "Leave it natural. We can pile it up on your head, maybe. Something messy but put together."

That's not how it's done. The words hovered on her tongue, damning and depressing. She didn't have to speak them—Lex would have caught her flash of confusion, and Lex would understand.

She met the older woman's eyes. Lex knew how a lifetime of lessons could wiggle under your skin, and that the things that hurt the worst weren't the ones everyone expected. They tiptoed around the women from Sector Two, whispering the word *whore* as if it was bad, as if being expected to sell their bodies was the worst thing that had happened to them.

"It gets easier, right?" She turned her hand and caught Lex's. Tried not to cling. "Remembering to have choices."

The woman's dark eyes gentled. "Eventually. But I'm not going to bullshit you. It took me a good, long while, and sometimes I still forget."

She didn't need it to be fast, as long as it was possible. Mia squeezed Lex's hand again before dropping to the edge of the bed. "It's not the worst thing in the world. Forgetting, I mean. Because every time I remember, it's like getting high on freedom all over again."

"Sounds like a good deal to me." Lex ducked into Ford's small bathroom, then emerged with a brush and a small bottle in her hand. "Knew he had to have some in there somewhere."

Conditioner, so new it still had a wrapper around the top. Not the custom handmade kind that was popular in Sector Two, but the kind produced in the factories of Sector Eight—where Ford had come from.

Mia felt a smile tugging at her lips. "I kind of

crashed on him last night. I'm surprised he dealt with it as well as he did."

Lex settled on the bed behind her and tore open the seal on the bottle. "Ford's no stranger to crisis. I think you might be his first damsel in distress, though."

"Really?" With that big heart beating under his grumpy exterior, Mia would have figured he'd have distraught women tossing themselves at him even without the handsome face and beautiful body. "I know he likes to scowl and snap, but it's just an act. Isn't it?"

"You may be underestimating the influence of your big eyes, honey."

Easy words. Mia turned them over, teasing apart the undertone. It hadn't sounded like an accusation, but her self-consciousness prompted a response. "I wasn't trying to play him. Not like that."

"Hey, I get it." Lex smoothed a tiny bit of the conditioner through Mia's hair. "A man like Ford? You can't play him with all those tricks Cerys teaches."

Lex's touch was gentle, soothing. Familiar, though she'd never known Lex personally. Mia could close her eyes, or even just squint a little, and it was like being back in the training house, relaxed in a way she could only be with her house sisters. Fixing hair, trading gossip, reveling in the rare liberty of not having to be perfect.

Maybe that was why it was suddenly easy to ask revealing questions. "What kind of man is he?"

"Stone cold," Lex answered without hesitation. "People get this idea in their heads of what that means—crazy, maybe. Can't feel anything. What it means to me is someone who'll do what he has to, no matter what."

Ford could feel, of that Mia had no doubt. But he wore that coldness like armor, and she could understand all the reasons a man might do that. Especially a man who felt vulnerable. "Like walking all the way back to the sector on a broken leg?"

"A damn fine example. Hand me that brush, would you?"

Mia passed it over her shoulder absently, her mind still struggling with the heartbreaking image. Derek, torn and bleeding, dragging himself back to Sector Four one agonizing step at a time. Stubborn as hell, but smart, too. She'd seen that intelligence. Not just in his eyes, but in his files. Paper was barbaric, but the things he'd written on it had revealed a cunning intellect and an ability not just to see the big picture, but to synthesize data and trends and extrapolate the least risky paths of expansion.

She could help him with that. Give him tools to automate the process, formulas that would unearth surprising patterns. Useless without human intelligence behind them, but the tech could do the tedious parts.

"I can assist him," she said, closing her eyes as Lex worked the brush through her hair. "I get what he's trying to do. Once I really understand the liquor, I can help."

"Is that what you want?"

"I want to be like you." The words slipped out, honest and awed, and warmth rushed to Mia's cheeks as she tried to modify the clumsy slip. "You and Jade, I mean. You're here, on your own terms. You're free. Where else can I be that?"

Lex chuckled. "I don't know, honey. Maybe a thousand places. Can't say for sure. But you're welcome to stay here."

Her next words couldn't be clumsy. They had to say the right thing—and *mean* the right thing. "Does how Ford feels about my big eyes matter for the job?"

"That depends. Do you like him?"

Another layered question. In Sector Two it covered a world of sins. *I like my patron* could mean tolerance, or contentment, or—in the rarest of cases—even honest affection. Or it could be a polite lie. "I like him," she replied carefully. "He's brusque, but that doesn't bother me. I think there's kindness in him. I'm...fond of him."

"Fond. Right." Lex patted her hip. "Turn around here for a second, huh?"

Tucking her leg up under her, Mia shifted on the bed to face Lex. The other woman was polished, perfect—and giving her an unmistakably knowing look. "Look, I'm the last woman to tell you not to get involved with an O'Kane. I *am* an O'Kane. But it's a hell of a hard road to walk. I'm not going to lie to you about that, either. So be sure you know what you want, okay?"

It was a warning, but it wasn't disapproval. Lex would never treat her like a broken doll in need of rescue. She'd lay out Mia's options, sometimes sharp enough for the edges to cut deep, but always honest. And then she'd stand back and expect Mia to use her brain and make her choices. Not just parroting the one Lex preferred, but having the spirit and stubbornness to go for what was best for *her*.

And Mia already knew what that was. "I want to prove myself. I don't even know what I can do, because no one's let me try."

"Dallas will." Lex said it with a steely conviction, not a shred of doubt intruding upon the words.

"And Ford?"

"What do *you* think?"

She'd seen the appreciation in his gaze at how easily she'd broken down his filing system and digitized the bulk of the data—but maybe she'd only wanted to see it. That appreciation could have been for her face and her body and how nice it was to have a pretty girl performing menial tasks. Even Vaughn had recognized the status symbol inherent in an aesthetically pleasing assistant.

Lex was still watching her, so Mia shrugged one shoulder. "I think it's hard to see people clearly when your heart gets in the way. When you want something to be real, you look for proof instead of truth."

"So you take your time," Lex said firmly. "It's the one thing that doesn't lie, right? Anyone can keep up bullshit, short term. But it gets harder as the clock ticks down."

Mia nodded her understanding and took a chance. "I need help to do this right. I think Ford doesn't want to overwhelm me, but I need to understand the liquor. I need to know all the variables."

"Then you talk to Dallas and Nessa." Her lips twisted into a wry smile. "Rachel, too, if you can find her. She's spending most of her time these days naked and sweaty, right between Ace and Cruz."

New names, people she'd have a chance to get to know if she found a place here. Dallas might be a little too intimidating for her first foray into the world of bootlegging, but today she'd be proactive. "Once I get myself put together, then, do you think you'd have time to introduce me to Nessa?"

"Sure." Lex grasped both her hands and peered down at them. "You can chat while she's doing your nails."

Mia started to flinch, then forced herself to relax with a wry laugh. "They never really let us see, do they? How much the illusion costs."

"Never. But, in Nessa's case, giving manicures is

something of a hobby." Lex tilted Mia's chin up with one finger. "Let her. The primping looks the same on the outside, maybe, but it's different. You're not dressing up to decorate some man. You're doing it to show everyone else in this sector that you can."

Because presentation was everything.

There was nothing new in the thought—she'd had it when Lex had walked in the door. But something inside Mia shifted, and the words looked different from this angle. She'd stared at Lex, aware of everything she represented and painfully aware of her own lack—but only because she wasn't used to being the one who lacked.

She should have realized. Especially since she was sitting on Ford's big, soft bed, his smooth sheets a sensuous whisper against her bare legs. *O'Kanes like our luxuries.* In Sector Two, Lex would have been one of the luxuries, a symbol that lifted the status of the man who owned her. A living reminder to everyone else—*this is what you'll never have.*

Lex wasn't a prize in Sector Four. She was the promise. The proof of how good life could be when you stood beside Dallas O'Kane. Not because you could aspire to have her.

You could aspire to *be* her.

"I understand," Mia said softly. "And thank you."

Lex hesitated. "You good?"

Maybe not yet, but she knew the answer now. She felt it in her bones. "I will be."

8

Mia looked like an O'Kane.

Ford stood in the office doorway and stared at her as she fluttered busily behind the desk. Her hair was smooth, and she was wearing jeans so tight they appeared to have been painted on, just like the polish on her nails.

Blood thundered in his ears as he closed the door behind him. "You've been busy."

"Hmm?" She glanced up from the tablet she held in one hand and blinked at him. "Oh, the outfit? Lex let me borrow some stuff. And then she took me to meet Nessa, who took me to meet her closet."

"I meant the..." He gestured to the files and notes covering the desk. "I didn't figure on you working today."

"Oh, that." Mia turned to sweep the scattered

papers covering one side into a haphazard pile. "Well, that's why Lex took me to meet Nessa. That girl knows a lot about liquor."

"She should. She makes it." The shirt Mia wore was made of some slinky, draped fabric, and slid away to bare her back when she leaned over. Ford swallowed hard.

"So I've learned. It was a pleasant surprise to find out that Dallas O'Kane's secret weapon is a nineteen-year-old..." She trailed off as she straightened, her gaze meeting his. A different sort of smile curved her lips, something sweet and still way too knowing. "Maybe I shouldn't have been shocked," she continued softly. "I know what young women can do."

"Yeah." Belatedly, he reached into his pocket and closed his hand around her battered locket. It was too light for its size—cheap and nickel-plated—and it almost tumbled from his palm as he held it out to her. "Here. They broke the chain, but you can get another one."

Her hand shook as she closed her fingers around it. "How did you find it?"

"Tracked down the bastards who took it. Wasn't hard."

Mia turned her hand and uncurled her fingers so slowly it was like she expected the locket to be gone. Her eyes were too bright, tears threatening, but she didn't cry as she brushed one fingertip around the edge. "Did you look inside?"

He'd figured it was damn well none of his business. "No, I didn't."

She worked a thumbnail under one edge and popped it open, holding it out so he could see. The picture inside was faded, small, but he could still make out the delicate features of a woman who shared Mia's dark skin, prominent cheekbones, and beautiful eyes.

"My mother," she whispered. "She died two years into my training, but she was sick before that."

His chest ached, and he wrapped one hand around the back of her neck. "I'm sorry."

"Don't be." She snapped it shut and fisted her hand. "You gave her back to me."

He ran his fingers up into her hair. "I got your jewelry back from a fence, that's all."

"Is that really all?"

Those big, warm eyes might chill when she found out the truth. "We also took care of the assholes who attacked your landlady. They won't be hurting anyone else."

But she only tilted her chin up, letting him cradle the back of her head as she smiled up at him. "You O'Kanes take care of your people."

"Always." His gaze settled on her lips, full and lush. Everything about her was lush, and he wanted her under him—her bare skin against his, hot moans sighing into his ear.

She wanted it, too. It was in every line of her body, in her too-quick breaths as her tongue darted over her lips. A heartbeat later she was gone, twisting back toward the desk in a flurry of nervous energy. "Nessa gave me what I needed to finish my program. More than I needed, really. I could only do the preliminary analysis, of course, but it will give us someplace to start."

Ford cleared his throat and dragged his libido under control. "Show me."

Visibly tense with nerves, Mia swept up the tablet

and handed it to him.

The application running on the tablet looked like a calculator, an interactive graph that updated its calculations as he changed quantities of ingredients—corn, wheat, and other grains as well as the rarer ingredients Nessa sometimes used. There were suggested figures based on their historical use, but every variable in the calculation could be manipulated.

"Cost analysis and potential profit," he summed up. "I'm impressed."

She lit up, her eyes sparking with enthusiasm as she reached out to swipe the screen to the second page. "I'm working on this, too—trying to factor in aging time and likely crop availability. It's more complicated than I ever realized, timing it so you have enough of everything."

"I'm not sure you could. Didn't Nessa give you her 'it's not a science, it's an art' speech?"

"She did, even though she'd just spent half an hour telling me how the science works." Mia reclaimed the tablet and smiled up at him. "I suppose the facts only get you so far, and the rest is a different sort of chemistry."

Another layer of meaning lurked beneath the words, but Ford only smiled and tapped his temple. "Most of this, I've got up here. It'll be good to have it someplace else, just in case. Thank you."

She wrinkled her nose as she gathered up her paperwork. "That's a criminal misuse of resources. You've got an amazing mind. It should be doing things tech can't do for you."

He placed his hand on the desk, pinning the papers to the surface as he leaned close to her ear. "Like what?"

Mia went still. Even her breath caught before she released it on a shaky sigh. "Thinking big thoughts."

"Is that really what *you're* thinking about right now?" he asked teasingly. "My big thoughts?"

She laughed, turning her face toward his cheek. Warm breath tickled his jaw, followed by the softest brush of her lips. "Yes. What else could possibly command my attention?"

"Lunch." He ran his free hand up her bare arm, relishing the thrill that stabbed through him when goose bumps rose at his touch.

"Lunch?"

Her distraction was gratifying. "Mmm. Unless you've already eaten."

"No, I got caught up in this." She tilted her head back against his shoulder, eyes closed, lips curving into a slow smile. "But I'm starving."

Ford stifled a groan. "Loaded words, buttercup. You ever rode a bike before?"

"Never."

"Ever had a real empanada?"

She turned in his arms to stare up at him, and all that hope was back in her eyes, along with a radiant curiosity. "No, I don't even know what that is."

"That's a damn shame." If he leaned down a few more inches, her mouth could be under his. He could be kissing her, picking her up and dropping her on his desk. Instead, he took a step back. "Get your coat."

For a flattering moment, she remained frozen, braced against the desk as if she'd been imagining the same thing. Her fingers traced back and forth over the wooden surface as her gaze swept up his body before fixing on his.

When she smiled, it lit her face with mischievous delight. "Are you going to take me for my first ride, Ford?"

"Uh-huh." He smiled back, slow and wicked. "But first, we're going for a spin on my new bike."

A quick, hard ride on Ford's desk would have satisfied her body, but a slow, easy ride on his bike healed her soul.

Maybe it was a whimsical thought, but there was more to the magic than the rumbling power of the bike between her thighs and the pleasure of snuggling up tight against Ford's back. The road stretching out ahead of them felt like freedom, even with the wind catching at her clothes, trying to hold her back.

It couldn't. Nothing could hold her back, not with Ford beside her.

Right now he was in front of her, blocking most of the wind with his massive shoulders. He'd spun them around the block a few times to let her get used to the feeling of being in the seat before gunning it for the edge of the sector, and Mia watched civilization fall away on either side of them. Well-kept buildings gave way to shabbier ones, which gave way to makeshift shelters built from whatever supplies their owners could find.

Sector Two was contained, enclosed inside a wall guarded by Cerys's carefully trained soldiers. Sector Four seemed to sprawl outward forever. There were even nicer buildings going up in the emptier spaces, wooden houses on neat lots, showing signs of care and effort.

She'd always known people flocked to Sector Four, and now she understood why. Dallas O'Kane was a benevolent dictator peddling hope, and nothing was at a higher premium these days.

They shot past the last line of buildings, and then freedom was more than just a feeling. It stretched out in front of them for endless miles, a cracked asphalt road disappearing into the distant horizon. And then Ford turned in a wide arc and they left even the road behind, speeding over the packed dirt as the wind stole her delighted laugh.

Maybe if they rode far enough, fast enough, the wind would rip away all the parts of Sector Two still clinging to her heart.

Ford was warm against her body, and she nestled closer as he pointed the bike toward a small cluster of buildings, more solid than most of the other shacks they'd passed. People milled around outside, shading their eyes to watch as she and Ford grew closer.

A settlement.

They coasted to a stop, and Mia pulled off the battered helmet Ford had found for her. It was easier to see without it, and there was so much to look at. Everything around her was makeshift but efficient—old train cars had been arranged so the backs formed part of the animal pen, and someone had hauled the seats out of a dozen cars and arranged them around a fire pit.

The adults were still watching them, silently respectful, but a little girl who couldn't have been more than ten broke away from her mother with an excited cry. "You got a new bike!"

"Sure did." Ford shut off the engine, kicked down the stand to stabilize the bike, and looked down at the girl. "Rachel just finished fixing it up for me. You like it?"

"Uh-huh." The girl circled the motorcycle, her big eyes transfixed. "I'll watch it for you, if you want. Are you here to see Dad?"

"Don't touch the exhaust," Ford warned as he climbed off the bike. "We're here to see your Aunt Lise."

"She's out back in her studio."

Mia slipped from the bike and set the helmet on the seat, hiding a smile as the girl shifted her weight from one foot to the other, nearly dancing with impatient energy. Sure enough, the words burst out before Mia had made it two steps away. "Hey, Ford! I can sit on it, right? I won't break it."

Ford tilted his head. "Depends. Does Shorty have anything left over in his truck from lunch, or did you greedy monsters wipe him out?"

The kid might have been small, but her shout echoed off the mountains. "Shorty! Ford wants some food."

A man with black hair, black eyes, and golden skin stuck his head out of the closest vehicle, an ancient delivery truck with peeling paint and a large window cut out of the side, and grinned widely. "Ford, you tough old bastard. Get over here."

Mia followed as Ford crossed the dusty clearing. Not so much as a hint of his limp showed in his careful but confident stride—not out here, not from the moment they'd set foot off O'Kane grounds.

No weakness, not in front of strangers.

Thank God she'd borrowed the clothing from Nessa. In the jeans and boots and wrapped tight in her new leather jacket, Mia wasn't presenting *her* version of perfection, but she could tell the image was the right one by the way the adult gazes followed her. More than one flicked to her wrists, and they'd made it most of the way to the trailer before she realized they were checking her for O'Kane ink.

Shorty braced his elbows on the dented metal ledge that had been welded onto the truck's makeshift window. "I got empanadas left, and some beans and rice. Who's the pretty lady?"

"This is Mia. She's a friend of Lex's."

"For a friend of Lex's, lunch is free." The cook grinned at her, and the expression looked right on his sun-weathered face. He had wrinkles, as if he smiled all the time. "It's been months since Lex came to visit. If you've got time, I can whip up a batch of tamales to take back to her. Tell her we miss her."

"Will do." Ford accepted the two beers Shorty passed through the window and tilted his head toward an empty wooden table nearby. "Let's have a seat."

The beer was ice-cold and far more bitter than the bottle she'd tried at the bar, but she took two long sips anyway, because trying new things felt like part of the adventure. And it *was* an adventure again—an even more exciting one than before.

Ford had given her that.

She smiled at him as she rubbed a thumb along the neck of the bottle. "Are there a lot of places like this? Not in the sectors, but not out in the communes, either?"

"Depends on where you go—and who's in charge."

"Is Dallas in charge all the way out here?"

"Yeah." Ford looked around, taking in the landscape, then gestured back in the direction of the city. "Technically, the sector border ends a ways back, but Dallas is a good leader. Tough but fair. He'll protect them, and he doesn't want trouble. That's enough to make the people here want to follow him."

They hadn't come far enough for the city to fall out of sight, though the dips and curves of the hills cut off the view of the sectors. From here only Eden was visible, the tops of the walls and the buildings that rose above them, some thirty or forty stories high. The sun caught the steel and reflected off windows, making the whole thing look like a desert mirage.

Eden, the impossible city. She'd lived in its shadow for so long that it felt disorienting to see it like this—a lonely cluster of buildings on the horizon, isolated in the middle of endless nothing.

The world was so much bigger than she'd ever dreamed.

It didn't take Shorty long to bring the food, and the empanadas turned out to be spicy meat encased in a flaky dough that melted on her tongue. She ignored proper etiquette and a lifetime of rules about when and how a lady ate, breaking off pieces with her fingers and making approving noises that weren't even a little bit seductive. "Why don't you have these for lunch all the time?"

Ford watched her, the corner of his mouth turned up in an easy smile that belied the heat in his eyes. "Because then it wouldn't be special."

"I don't believe you. You could eat these every day and they'd still be special."

"That's the truth, because I *do* eat them every day," said a new voice, and a pretty brunette with battered jeans, a messy ponytail, and a leather apron dropped into an empty chair. "Ford, good to see you out and about. I heard you were looking for me."

"Mia, this is Lise." He wiped his mouth with his napkin and pulled his cigarette case out of his pocket. "She makes jewelry."

"Among other things." She held out her hand. "Nice to meet you."

Mia held out her own hand as the connection fell into place. "Stuart's sister? I think I saw some of your work in the market when Trix took me shopping for my coat. You're very skilled."

"Thanks." Lise slanted a sidelong look at Ford before smiling. "So what can I do for you?"

Mia slipped her locket out of her pocket and set it on the table. "I know it's not much, but it means a lot to me. Ford said you'd be able to find a new chain."

"You need more than that." Lise flicked her thumbnail over the loop at the top of the locket. It was bent and twisted, one side broken clean through. "But I can fix it. You'll be here for a while?"

Ford grunted in confirmation.

Lise rose. "Consider it done."

And that was that. Lise swept away, locket in hand, and Mia only briefly considered asking about money before letting it go. For all she knew, Lise would perform the task for free because Ford was an O'Kane, and that meant something even out here.

"Thank you," she said instead, slipping her hand over his. "For this. For everything. Just...thank you."

He turned his hand, his fingers twining with hers, but he remained silent for so long she thought he wouldn't speak. Then he met her gaze. "It's important to you. That makes it important to me."

Oh *God*.

It was unfair, really. The man should have to work for it—a wink or a smile or something—not just sit there staring at her with dark eyes and a stony expression that turned her flight toward freedom into a dizzying, exhilarating fall.

He'd catch her every time, and all she had to do in return was let him. Let him be her safety net, let him sand off the rough, uncomfortable parts of freedom. It wouldn't have to be like Sector Two all over again. She could be like this settlement—giving her loyalty freely because she got so much in return.

Ford would demand plenty. He'd sweep through

her life on a wave of protective fury, giving her all the things he wanted her to have, washing away anyone who threatened her. She could only imagine the games he'd play with her in bed—her body heated at the thought of being at his mercy. He'd be possessive and bossy and exasperating, all three, every day.

But he'd give back a hundred times what he took. He'd give her affection and pleasure and a chance to use her wits and her brains and her skills for something bigger than herself.

He'd care, and that was the oddest feeling of all. Being cared for.

He was still watching her, handsome and brooding and perfect, so she leaned in and lowered her voice to a whisper. "Watch out, Derek. I'm starting to suspect you like me a little bit."

Instead of answering, he lifted her hand and brushed a kiss across her knuckles.

Oh yeah. She was falling. And she never wanted to stop.

9

Dallas O'Kane's weekly fight night should have been as far from the sedate civilization of Sector Two as it was possible to travel, but being surrounded by O'Kane women as they gossiped and cheered was like coming home.

Lex had recreated the best part of Sector Two, stripped of competition and desperation. Sisterhood, raw and pure, and Mia was drunk on it from the moment Nessa dragged her down to a couch.

"Just wait," Nessa promised, passing her a shot glass. "These are just some punk kids warming the place up. Wait until our boys get in the cage. Jas or Bren or Cruz..."

"Cruz is busy," Lex corrected, grinning. "He disappeared into Ace's room with Rachel—and locked the door behind him."

"Ace is missing fight night? *Shit.* The sex must be supernova hot." Nessa snatched up a shot of her own and knocked it back before giving Mia an expectant look. Remembering the last time she'd hit the whiskey too hard, Mia took a sip.

A small one.

She nearly spit it back out again when Noelle appeared. Most of the O'Kane women owned a style that could best be described as sex edged with danger, but Noelle had abandoned the leather and denim she'd worn while working the bar in favor of the sort of dress a Rose might wear—lacy, white, and short enough to flash the delicate garters sitting high on her thighs.

Noelle looked like innocence begging to be debauched, and the glint in her eyes as she dropped into Lex's lap proved she knew it. She kissed Lex's cheek before grinning at Nessa. "Don't worry, Jas is fighting later, and Bren's getting in the cage in a little bit. Mia will have the full O'Kane fight night experience."

But Ford wouldn't be fighting. He was leaning against the wall near the bar, his attention trained on the two men brawling in the cage. Her heart beat faster when she looked at him, and not just because he was gorgeous even in jeans, his shirt stretched tight over every perfect muscle in his chest and shoulders.

He still hadn't taken her. The tension stretching out between them had skittered past anticipation that afternoon, settling low in her body as an ache that wouldn't ease until he was inside her, stoking a different sort of need.

But Nessa had been waiting for them in Ford's office, touchingly excited to offer Mia her spare bed for as long as Mia wanted to stay...and Ford hadn't murmured a word of protest. He'd even seemed eager to have her safely settled elsewhere.

So she'd gone, because perhaps he wanted her to know her safety wasn't tied up in his bed. He wanted her to come back because she *wanted* to, not because she had nowhere else to go.

Or maybe he'd just wanted to get her out of his hair. That was the possibility that kept her rooted to the couch instead of crossing the crowded room to talk to him.

"Mia!"

Fingers snapped in front of Mia's face, and she started, turning to look in Nessa's direction. Her gaze snagged on Lex and Noelle, who were stroking each other in a way that brought a flush to Mia's skin. Casual physical affection—another perk of living in Sector Two, one she'd lost when she'd left Orchid House for Vaughn's sterile, lonely estate.

Nessa laughed and nudged Mia with her shoulder. "Don't mind them. They're just real friendly."

"I don't mind at all." Mia met Lex's gaze and smiled. "It's a little like home. The good parts of it."

"Mmm." Lex blinked innocently. "They don't have men like Ford in Sector Two, though."

No, they really didn't. She snuck another peek at him, tracing the line of his jaw and the stern set of his brow. He always looked so serious, but she'd learned to find the warm places in him, edges that softened just for her. "Is this something he did before the accident? Fight in the cage?"

"Nah, he hasn't been around much. Hopefully that'll change now."

"That's the plan anyway," a new voice rumbled, and Mia followed a pair of leather pants up to a wide belt buckle, and over endless skin covered in beautiful tattoos before reaching Dallas O'Kane's eyes.

She knew it was him, even though this was the

first time she'd laid eyes on Sector Four's infamous leader. There was no one else it *could* be—and not only because everyone within twenty feet was slowly turning, as if his mere presence drew them in like gravity. The tattoo that stretched across his collarbone and climbed up his throat was a stylized version of the O'Kane logo beneath an intricate crown—the twin of the one Lex wore, and decorated with her name.

He held out a hand, and Lex dragged him down into a hungry kiss. Their tongues flashed, but it was Noelle who moaned, low and shaky—and Mia realized that Lex and Dallas's joined hands had slid up under the woman's dress.

It was shameless, casual and easy, as if it happened all the time—and maybe it did, because Nessa rolled her eyes and did another shot. "That's how Lex and Dallas say *hi*. You get used to it."

Dallas laughed and slipped his hand out from under Noelle's skirt. Even in the uncertain light, Mia could see that his fingertips were slick with arousal. He traced one over Noelle's parted lips with a smile. "You sure got used to it, didn't you, kitten?"

Noelle nipped his finger. "Only when it gets me in trouble. Have you met Mia yet?"

That dark, dangerous gaze swung toward her, and for the first time in her anything-but-innocent life, Mia felt utterly out of her depth. Sex was everywhere in Sector Two. Affection between the girls, training in the houses, provided to patrons. She knew chapter and verse when it came to vices, lists of sexual positions, and techniques that had seemed dry and impersonal, even when she was watching them play out before her.

Chilly. Everything in Two had been cool, calculated. Heat radiated off Dallas and Lex and everyone around them, and Mia's heart raced out of control as she struggled for a casual tone. "I'm honored."

"Are you, now?" Dallas straightened slowly. "I hear you've been turning Ford's life upside-down."

Nerves left her lips numb, as if she'd had as much to drink as Nessa instead of one tiny sip. This was *Dallas O'Kane*, the man whose viciousness and ruthlessness kept everyone in the sector safe. And he was staring down at her, his fingers still thrusting between Noelle's lips with an absent-minded lewdness that bordered on obscene.

No, it *was* obscene. And it was making that hungry ache inside Mia worse.

She wet her lips and hid her nervousness with a bright smile. "I don't know about his life. Mostly his filing system. I can't believe he was wasting his time with paper records."

The wrong words. Mia's heart stopped as Dallas's face twisted into a scowl—an intimidating, terrifying scowl that slammed down on her like the weight of the entire sector. She barely heard Noelle erupt into giggles—the sound was meaningless with all that danger and irritation burning through her.

Then Dallas snorted. "Great. I'm fucking surrounded. Way to make me feel old, Lex."

She wrapped her fingers around his belt buckle and gave it a teasing tug. "You'll live."

Mia's pulse slowed. A little. "I'm sorry if—"

Noelle cut her off with a laugh. "No, don't apologize to him. He doesn't deserve it."

"Watch it, kitten," Dallas growled. "You get too mouthy, and I'll tell Jas not to spank you tonight."

"Then we'd all be sad." Lex eased Noelle off her lap, rose, and whispered something in his ear.

Whatever it was, it must have been filthy. Dallas groaned and claimed Lex's mouth in another of those hard, messy kisses, one so raw and carnal Mia felt her own body react. God, she'd seen shows designed to titillate that contained less passion than this spontaneous, shameless kiss.

In the end, she had to look away. But that only made the confusion churning inside of her worse, because Ford was making his way across the room, his gaze fixed on her.

He stopped beside the raised platform that held the couches. "Ladies. Dallas."

"Ford." It was Dallas's voice, low and lazy. "Are you here to rescue your woman? She's looking a little dazed already, and Lex hasn't even crawled under Noelle's skirt yet."

Ford didn't blink. "I thought you might like the grand tour, Mia."

Fleeing was nothing short of cowardice—and she was okay with that. "I'd love a tour," she said quickly, hopping off the couch and then the stage. She landed next to Ford with a wobble, and if she heard Dallas laughing behind her...

Better laughing than growling.

Ford tucked her hand around his bent elbow and led her away. "Does he frighten you?"

"Yes," she admitted. She might tease Ford about always getting his way, but one look into Dallas O'Kane's eyes and anyone with wits would know the truth—Dallas was a man who never had to settle for the word *no*. "No wonder Cerys loathes him."

Ford arched one eyebrow. "When it comes to people, he doesn't take things by force. He doesn't have to."

That only made him more dangerous. The other sector leaders might force you into a cage. Cerys would do her damnedest to trick you. But Dallas could make you walk into captivity and hand him the key with your own two hands. "I'm not worried he'll hurt me," she said quietly, tightening her grip on Ford's arm. "He's just...intimidating."

"Because you don't know him like I do." Ford sighed. "You should have seen him in the early days. He never wanted to be a king, not really, but it's the best way for him to keep this sector safe."

"I think I understand." How could she not, with the crowd parting in front of Ford as he led her back toward the bar? The ink on his wrists wasn't magic, after all. It drew its power from Dallas, from his reputation, and he had to be intimidating to be strong enough to protect anyone whose life brushed his.

"It's a show." Ford slowed to a stop near the cage, his voice pitched low but carrying easily enough under the raucous din. "Not all of it. Not the life. But there are some things about it an outsider will never see. Hell, some things it's taken *me* a while to see."

She shivered as a shout of pain drew her gaze to the fight. She didn't recognize either of the men taking swings at each other, but there was something intimate even in their anonymity. It was a different way to be naked, violence stripping away everything but the base desire to survive.

On the couches they'd left behind, a different sort of base desire was playing out. Noelle and Lex again, seemingly oblivious to the attention they were stealing from the fight as they exchanged lazy kisses and touches. Goose bumps shivered up Mia's arms, and she rubbed at them lightly and forced her attention away. "I thought..."

She trailed off, unsure if it was rude to ask, unsure what she'd do with the answer. Everyone knew Noelle had hooked up with Dallas's right-hand man, but she wasn't acting like an owned woman—unless Dallas and Lex shared ownership of everyone who wore ink.

Ford glanced back and huffed out a laugh. "Don't worry—Dallas and Jas are down with it."

"It's different," Mia admitted, leaning into his side and telling herself it was for the warmth, as if the heat of the lights and the crowd weren't more than enough to counteract the evening chill. "I'm starting to think I don't know very much about sex at all. Not the kind people have together."

"When they both want it, you mean?"

Not just that. Her gaze drifted back to Lex and Noelle, and she recognized those touches. She'd touched other women like that, and had been touched in return. There'd been comfort in the intimacy, and true desire. But every caress had been stolen, laced with tension and worry, because your body wasn't yours to give. And if you gave too much to the wrong person...

"The kind you have when you're allowed to want it," she corrected softly. "I've never been that free. They're not performing, but they don't need to hide. Because they can do anything they want."

"So can you." Ford slid his hand under her hair and wrapped it around the back of her neck. "You don't ever have to go back there."

Desire crept through her, starting in the oddest places. Her fingertips tingled. Her toes curled in her borrowed boots. His hand felt dangerous and protective, resting at the top of her spine, and she felt the dichotomy in every inch of her body. She barely heard the crowd roar as the fight in front of her spun its way to a violent conclusion.

Every molecule in her body was focused on where he'd touch her next.

His thumb stroked up the side of her throat, all

the way to the spot just behind her ear.

Mia shivered and let her eyelids droop, shutting out the new fighters climbing into the cage as well as the crowd around them. "Tell me what you see in them. The things you didn't notice at first."

"Trust. Dedication. Love." The word blew hot over her lips. "This isn't just my job. It's my family."

Envy stole her breath. She was greedy, because she wanted all of it. Him, his mind, his body, the chance to work beside him—

They were so close now, so close she could lean up and her lips would brush his. "I'm jealous. I feel like I've been alone forever."

"Do you feel alone here? Now?"

"Not when you're touching me."

"Then I won't stop." His hand slipped around, nudging her locket before dropping lower. "Unless you ask me to."

His knuckles grazed the skin bared by her plunging neckline, stroking between her breasts, and her pulse pounded in her ears, drowning out the sound of the new fight. He was touching her, caressing her in the middle of a crowd, but even though her skin prickled with awareness, one glance around them made it clear no one was staring.

Maybe the fight was too exciting, or the sight of a man teasing his fingers over a woman's body was too tame to merit notice. Or maybe no one would dare gawk at Ford even if he bent her over the nearest table and took her on the spot, because that was the power of being an O'Kane.

She tilted her head back, letting her eyes drift shut as she floated on the energy of the crowd and the sensation of his fingers. "Please don't stop."

His touch ventured beneath the fabric of her shirt

and followed the inner curve of her breast. "How far, Mia?"

Only one answer to give. The only one that mattered here in the heart of O'Kane territory. "I trust you."

Ford moved, nudging Mia until she hit something hard that dug into the middle of her back—the bar. Glass clinked as he leaned over her, his mouth close to her ear. "Do you care if people watch? Do you want them to?"

"What other people?" She slid her hands up over those gorgeous arms to the broad shoulders that blocked out the rest of the world. "I only see you."

He lifted his hand to her chin and turned her head toward the couches on the platform.

The O'Kanes dared to watch.

A man had taken Mia's abandoned place on the couch, one with massive shoulders and a full beard, and his fingers tangled casually in Noelle's hair. He and Lex were taking turns toying with Noelle's body while all three of them stared at Ford and Mia, and the illusion of invisibility vanished.

"Oh," she whispered, clutching at his shoulders. "Do *you* care?"

His jaw clenched, a muscle ticking as he stared down at her. He took a step back—mere inches, but it felt like *miles*—and grabbed her hand.

"Come on," he growled. "Let's go."

Oh yes, Ford cared—and not about being seen with his hands under his assistant's clothing. He was a marvel of possessive hunger, his gaze so intense people scrambled out of their path as he tugged her toward the door, and Mia almost laughed at the sheer relief.

She'd be in Ford's bed again soon, and this time she wouldn't be alone.

10

For an O'Kane, sex was everything and nothing, all at once.

It was everything because it meant freedom, not only from expectations but from the twisted morality that Eden held so dear. Here, there was a different culture at work, one that celebrated physicality and pleasure. Affection and release.

And nothing—nothing because until there was a commitment involved, promises and collars and marks, it was all casual. An O'Kane had to be ready to walk when the sun rose, content in the knowledge that everyone involved had had a damn good time.

This was different.

He crossed the threshold and stopped in the darkness just inside his bedroom, but he didn't turn to look at Mia. Not yet. He stared at the bed instead, picturing her dark hair spread across the pillow, her lips and thighs parted. Waiting for him.

Fabric rustled behind him. A boot thumped against the floor, then a second. She was reaching for her shirt as he turned, but her hands stilled on the hem, fingers bunching the fabric. "I wasn't trained to be submissive. I need you to know that."

Training. For a moment, the thought of it was almost enough for rage to overwhelm his lust. Then he focused on the bare strip of skin just above her pants, and everything else dissolved.

He reached for her shirt, pulling the fabric out of her hands as he drew it up to reveal even more luscious skin. "It's not something to train for. It's not a job. You like it or you don't, that's all."

"You don't understand." She clutched his hand hard enough for her fingers to dig in as she met his eyes. "I know what submission is. It's everything I was never allowed to have, because my job was to manage every moment without letting him see my power. When I give you control, I need you to know I understand what I'm doing. That I'm making a choice, because I want to."

Precious, fragile—not her, but the moment. So Ford nodded. "I'll take it if you want to give it to me. But I don't need it, Mia."

"Maybe only sometimes." She traced her fingertips up his arm, ghosting along his throat and jaw before touching his lips. "Maybe tonight. This is the fantasy I never dared have."

Then he'd give her one she wouldn't forget. He drew her shirt up higher, lingering over the fullness of her breasts, rubbing the satiny fabric over the tight peaks of her nipples.

Her breath caught, eyelids fluttering shut as she

lifted her arms. "What *do* you need?"

The words came without thought. "Tonight," he whispered. "Let me show you."

"Anything." She shivered as he stripped her shirt away, but not with nerves. When her gaze met his again, he saw only hunger and need. "God, Derek. *Everything*. I want you to show me everything."

All the things she'd been missing. Ford seized one lock of hair and teased it over her bare shoulder. "It could take a while."

"I'm not going anywhere." She tilted her head to the side, practically begging him to move his caress up the side of her neck. "I think I like Sector Four."

Good. He didn't say it aloud. She was flying high on the seductive lure of the O'Kane lifestyle, not to mention her first real taste of freedom, and only an asshole would take advantage of that to lock her in to something permanent.

But he could still fulfill her fantasy—ownership without begrudging lust or regret. Without punishment. So instead of tickling her hair up the delicate line of her throat, he leaned in and bit her.

She moaned. Swayed. Her hands flew up to grasp his shoulders, fingers digging in desperately. "Oh God, I like that, too."

"Uh-huh." He licked a path up to her ear and bit her again.

Another moan. Her grip tightened until his shirt seemed in danger of ripping. "How many places are you going to bite before you're inside me?"

"You want me to keep count?"

"Maybe." She shifted one hand to his belt, tugging at the leather, fumbling to get it open. "I don't know, I just—I *want*."

He locked his fingers around her wrist. "Mia, look

at me."

Shivering, she lifted her gaze.

She was spinning, reaching out for anything that would calm her nerves, but only one thing would work. "Trust me."

"I do," she whispered. "But it's the first time. And it shouldn't be a big deal, because I'm not innocent. But they made it one. They made it the only thing about me that matters, and sometimes I just want it over with."

He stared at her for a moment before he realized what she was talking about. "Honey, getting a dick inside you is only part of sex, not all of it."

"I know," she protested, but then she let her head fall forward, burying her face in his chest with a groan. "I knew. I let them get to me. And then I let *you* get to me. I can't stop thinking about your dick."

He might have laughed, if his dick hadn't taken such a keen interest in her admiration. He reached for the button on her pants and backed her toward the bed. "In good time, buttercup."

"I trust you." It sounded stronger this time, like an offer instead of a reassurance. She helped him strip away her pants before resting one knee on the bed. "Is this where you want me?"

"Stop." He stepped up behind her. She was wearing tiny black panties edged with a hint of lace, and he eased his hand beneath them to rest on her bare hip. "Stop asking, stop talking. Just stop."

She went still. Nodded.

He turned her around and tugged his shirt over his head. Then he held her gaze as he dropped his hands to his belt and unbuckled it. Silence stretched out between them, broken only by ragged breathing and her gasp when he pulled her fingers to the top button of his jeans.

She didn't fumble this time. She went slowly, working the buttons free one at a time, her eyes never leaving his. When she was done, he captured her wrists again, eased her down to the bed, and finished undressing.

Her gaze skittered away from him, nervous and uncertain, because watching was new. She'd always been the object of lust, never the one allowed to indulge. But after a few heartbeats of hesitation she clutched at the covers and looked straight at him, eyes meeting his for a grateful moment before her focus wandered.

She stared at his chest. Lingered on his shoulders. She spent forever working her way down his arm to his hand, but from there her gaze swept straight to his cock.

And stayed.

His cock jumped as blood roared in his ears. "So hungry," he murmured. "Time to stop asking, Mia, and start taking."

She parted her lips, but instead of speaking, she caught the lower one between her teeth. It took forever for her to rise to her knees, to inch to the edge of the bed, until she could reach out and trace her fingertips over his chest.

Her fingers followed the outline of his tattoo, her touch a teasing graze that grew bolder as she drifted down. She spread her hand wide against his abdomen with a wondering smile. "You're going to make me greedy."

That smile hit him in the gut. "You should be. Who the hell wants to be delicate and shy about sex?"

"No one," she whispered, and closed her hand around his cock.

Heat sizzled up his spine as she stroked him—once, twice—and then dropped her gaze, her lip trapped between her teeth again as she watched her hand smooth back down to the base of his shaft. "This is what I can't stop thinking about. How big you'll feel inside me."

"We'll go slow." Or not, if her passion conquered the discomfort. She might beg him to go faster, to give her more, and that was the thought that drove him to the bed.

He pushed her back and stretched out beside her, toying with the edge of her panties as he wound his other hand in her hair. She arched, dropping one trembling hand to cover his. But only for a moment, because this time she didn't ask.

She took.

Her hand slipped past his, under the fabric of her panties, and she met his eyes with her first soft moan.

Ford groaned. "That's right." He pulled her panties down, baring her fingers and her pussy to his sight. "Take it, sweetheart."

Her eyes fluttered shut as she lifted her chin, digging her head back into the blankets. She opened her legs, giving him a better view as she spread her fingers to part her pussy lips. Her middle finger swept in a lazy circle, up and down, around and around, close enough to her clit to make her squirm but never quite touching.

She liked the tease. Ford hummed his approval and nipped at the soft skin beneath her chin. "Faster," he whispered.

Moaning, she dipped her finger lower, rocking it into her body before coming back to touch the slick fingertip to her clit. Her breath hissed out, and she shook her head. "It's too good."

"Yeah?" He shifted on the bed, easing down to

drop his next gentle bite to her hip.

Her fingers froze, and she shuddered. "Make me feel it." Not a command but a plea, and she was practically begging as she shoved at the fabric tangled around her hips. "I'll run from the pleasure if you let me. Don't let me."

"Shh." He guided her panties down her mile-long legs and settled between them as he smoothed his hands back up to her thighs. "That's the only way I know how to do this, Mia. Nothing held back."

"Nothing held back," she echoed, letting her arms fall to her sides. "I took what I wanted. Now let me take what you want."

"Don't move," he warned, holding her open with his fingers as his breath blew across her slick flesh. Then, before she could respond, he circled her clit with his tongue—close, but not quite touching, just the way she'd touched herself at first.

She didn't move—not really—but she squirmed. Her thighs tensed against his shoulders and she dragged in a ragged breath. "Yes. *Yes.*"

He grazed her clit with the rough pad of his thumb, then soothed it with his tongue.

That made her move. She whimpered and jerked her hips, as if trying to escape the contact. Ford held her still for one more direct caress, then lapsed into lazy exploration.

Her squirming subsided, but her noises didn't. Soft at first, just breathy sighs and the occasional moan. She seemed content to float on pleasure for a while, but the tension returned to her body when he maintained an easy pace.

She tried to move again then, *toward* him this

time, and she bit off a muttered curse when he stopped her. "Derek."

"Not yet." She was wet but tight, so tight that even one finger stretched her when he pushed it slowly inside.

"Oh, *God*." Her fingers tangled in his hair, yanking as her body clenched around him. "Even your fingers are big. I love them."

Hot, impossibly hot. "Not as big as my cock." Somehow he knew she'd melt around him then, too, when he was over her, pressing her down into the mattress, sliding into her for the first time.

"I know, God, I know..." She rocked up, forcing his finger deeper. "I've imagined it. The first night I met you, I went home and imagined you."

Ford groaned again and froze, stilling his hand as he looked up at her. "Tell me."

"You offered to take out your dick right there in the office." She laughed breathlessly, tugging at his hair. "I closed my eyes and pretended you had. Men have jerked off because of me before, but never for me. In my fantasy, you did it just for me."

"You like that idea?" He withdrew from her slowly, bit by bit, and gave her two fingers this time in a teasing thrust that barely breached her entrance.

"*Yes*," she hissed, and it could have been an answer or sheer relief. She pulled at his hair again, lifting her hips with a pleading noise. On edge now, her pussy gripping his fingers, drawing them deeper.

So Ford gave her what she wanted, a slow, inexorable invasion with just enough time to adjust, but not enough to flinch away. Not that she was trying anymore—every slip in her restraint brought her closer, taking everything he offered and begging for more.

After the first whimper, he lowered his mouth—lashing his tongue over her clit, fucking her with his fingers—and listened to her cries begin to rise.

Mia was flying apart.

Ford was crude. He was brazen. He had two big, blunt fingers pumping into her body, working her open, and it was the *sound*—slick and hot and shameless—that made her want to fling her hands over her burning cheeks.

She'd never been this wet before. She'd never been this far past caring about anything but release, and still Ford strung her along, twisting his fingers until they went from *too big* to *not enough*, swiping his tongue over again and again but never lingering, never giving her what she needed to soar.

"More," she moaned.

"More of what, sweetheart?" His voice had dropped to a growl, and he flicked his tongue over her again. "More of that? Or more of this?" He withdrew his fingers only to return immediately with another, three blunt fingers stretching her wide.

It hurt, but only a little, and even that vanished under another rush of frustrated need. He could have made her come a dozen times by now, but he was playing her body. Coaxing her into a state of such desperation that nerves and discomfort and anxiety didn't exist.

Pleasure did. This sweet agony of hanging just short of orgasm. She clutched at his head with both hands now, chanting his name and pleas as she tried to get closer to his tongue, but he was unshakable. Nothing about this moment and what was to come rested on her actions, and that was the most dizzying realization of all.

She didn't have to manage this. It was all for her.

He growled again, his mouth on her, and this time the sound vibrated through her, shivering across every overstimulated nerve.

So close. So *close*. Every muscle in her body knew it, and it had to be instinct, some ancient fucking wisdom imparted in her cells because nothing in her life or training had prepared her to feel so open, so ready, so hot and hungry.

Her body knew. Everything twisted inward, tensing for a heartbeat that stretched on for a lifetime.

Then he curled his fingers inside her, and she really did fly apart.

She fell forever. This wasn't some quiet orgasm, release slipping over with the gentleness of her own touch. Ford hadn't been gentle. He'd pushed her hard, worked her over, dragging her through a frustration she never would have had the patience to inflict upon herself, which was a pity because the reward—

Oh God, the reward. Everything shuddered and pulsed, her pussy clenching tight, forcing her to feel the broad fingers still stroking into her, still coaxing. And that was another way she'd been failing herself, because her focus waned with release.

His didn't.

She didn't just come. She kept coming, driven on by his growls and his tongue and the fingers that refused to relent. Not even when she panted his name and tried to squirm away, because it was too much, too good, and she hadn't worked for this, hadn't earned it—

Make me feel it, she had pleaded, and he did, and

she loved him a little bit for it.

No wonder blowjobs made men so stupid.

He bit her again, a rough, bruising caress on her inner thigh. "You're fucking beautiful."

The kiss of pain licked up her spine, splitting the overwhelming press of bliss into manageable pieces. Still panting, she pulled weakly at his hair, trying to urge him up her body. "Be in me. I want you in me."

Ford loomed over her, his eyes dark, his muscles tense and trembling. "Now?" he asked, his voice deadly quiet as he flexed his hips, nudging her with his erection.

It would hurt, but she needed it. Needed him, and it wasn't about symbolic virginity or the need to be rid of it, not anymore. It was about the empty ache where his fingers had been and the need to see her dazed pleasure reflected in his eyes.

She slid her hands down his body, over his broad shoulders, his smooth back, to his hips, where she dug her fingers into his skin and pulled him closer. "Do you want me to say it like an O'Kane would? Take me, Ford. Fuck me."

He shifted, and the head of his cock pushed against her entrance. He lifted his thumb to her lips. "Say it again."

His skin tasted like her. She licked him. Shivered. She could already imagine him surging inside her, plunging so deep she'd feel him for days. "Fuck me, Derek. Pl—"

He cut her off with a kiss—and a slow, unyielding thrust.

She expected pain, braced for it. But she was so wet, still melting from his fingers, so close to ready. Her body stretched to accommodate him, welcoming him as he worked deeper and deeper—

And deeper.

And *deeper.*

The stretch became an ache, became something sharper still, and she whimpered against his mouth, her confidence momentarily shaken. She was already so full, she couldn't take more, no matter how much she wanted him. He was too big, too much, too everything.

And then he was fully seated, still, his panting breaths his only movement. He licked her tongue, swallowed her whimper, and raised his head. "Okay?"

Poor Ford. He looked like he was the one in agony, and she knew he must be. If he felt impossibly big to her, her body must be impossibly tight, clenching hot and wet around him. But he hovered above her, muscles standing out in stark, tense relief, every bit of focus fixed on her.

Ford would hurt himself before he hurt her, so she dug her nails into his back and lifted her hips with a moan. "I will be when you're fucking me."

His breath caught. "You won't be thinking that for long if I don't give you a minute here, trust me."

She could tell him she'd been trained for this. Trained to compartmentalize the pain, to show only the flattering bits—*oh, you're so big, I can't take you, no wait, I think I like it, fuck me harder*—but it would have been a lie.

She'd been trained to fake it, not to feel it. She couldn't break down these sensations and shove them into neat, contained boxes. The pain was part of the pleasure, the pleasure part of the pain.

She wanted them both, messy and real, so she flexed her fingers again. "Trust *me.* I'll tell you if it's too much, I promise. But let me take this. Let me take you."

Ford gave in, every muscle flexing as he thrust

against her, and any hope of containment slipped away. Because pleasure and pain could be managed, but the intimacy of staring up into his face as the grip of her body tore away his restraint...

She'd wrecked him. Not by plying him with fancy tricks, not by withholding or granting favors. She'd offered him control, and had taken something deeper in exchange, something she didn't have a word for but could see plainly in his eyes as he rolled forward again.

It drove a gasp from her lips. Surprise, because the places that had ached were doing something else now, heating up with the friction of his thrusts. It made her want more, made her arch and strain into him, breathlessly anticipating that moment where he slammed deep and something wild sparked inside her.

He did it again, harder this time, and threw his head back with a curse. "Fuck. *Fuck.*"

She would have echoed him if she'd had the breath to, but that spark had flared briefly into flame, and she needed it again. Needed it or she'd die, so she whimpered and pulled at him, trying to urge him to go faster. Harder. *Something.*

"Don't want to hurt you—" He snarled and rolled over onto his back, bringing her on top of him. He locked his hands around her rib cage and urged her upright. "Like this."

Her knees splayed wide, falling to the mattress on either side of his body, and gravity did the rest. She cried out as his cock drove even deeper, grasping at his forearms as he steadied her. "Oh, oh *fuck.*"

Ford dropped his hands to her hips and lifted her just a little. "Easy, love. Easy."

"Derek." His grip was steel, refusing to let her sink back down, and she smacked her palms to his chest and gave him a warning taste of her nails. "I don't want easy. I want to feel you."

"Yeah?" He arched up, a slow roll that he pulled her down to meet. It didn't stop, just flowed into another movement, their bodies rising and falling together.

She caught the rhythm. Matched it. Tried to speed it, and groaned when he tightened his fingers, keeping control, forcing her to feel every inch of his advance and withdrawal again and again.

Since she couldn't match him in physical strength, she fought with words—because calling it that sounded less desperate than begging. "I need your cock. Please, Derek. Please, give it to me. Let me take it."

"You don't *need* it, not yet." He let her slide down into his next thrust, then eased his hand around to the front of her body. His thumb centered on her clit, tracing slow circles, increasing the pressure with every rock of his hips. "But you will."

He was right. She didn't need his cock enough to move away from the dizzying circle his thumb was making. He could control her movements with just that one point of contact, and she didn't care anymore because she was going to come again, come harder, shaking apart right on top of him while he watched and reveled in it.

"That's right." He gritted his teeth as she shuddered. "You know what comes next, don't you, sweetheart?"

"I do," she whispered. Maybe she did. She couldn't hear her own words over her pulse, because she could feel her heartbeat everywhere. In her head, in her fingers and toes, centered at her clit while he rubbed and rubbed.

Her gaze locked onto his, and God, the approval there, the fierce pleasure, as if he'd never seen anything as wonderful as her shaking apart on his cock.

He wanted her just like this, a filthy, greedy goddess, one who told him exactly what she wanted, how fast and how deep, how rough and how raw.

He wanted her to come, and she did. Hard, the pleasure so intense she could only moan helplessly as she rode his dick and his hand. And he let her, let her take what she wanted. Let her take what she needed.

Let her take *him*.

She was as dizzy from that as she was from the shuddering pleasure, which went on and on until she was swaying above him, her nails digging into his skin.

He caught her. Steadied her. His fingers curled tight around her hips, and she felt the balance shift, even though they'd barely moved. She could feel it in his grip, see it in his eyes.

It was Ford's turn to take.

He dragged her down to his chest and held her there, one huge hand splayed between her shoulder blades. The position pulled her hips up, leaving him to cover the distance between them with a powerful thrust.

She turned her cheek to his neck, nuzzling against him with an approving moan. So many words hung on the tip of her tongue—*yes* and *more* and *harder*—but she set her teeth in his skin instead.

Marking him. Trusting him.

His other hand settled on the curve of her ass, then dipped lower, stroking over her pussy where she stretched wide around his cock. "So wet," he hissed.

"Because it's good." She lifted her head and caught his gaze. "Because I want your cock. Do you like hearing that?"

"I like feeling it." He moved his hand as he spoke, slicking his fingers up to tease between her ass cheeks. And she knew the practicalities of that, too, all the ways she could prepare herself to handle a man who wanted to put his dick somewhere else, but this was different. Just a tease, stroking untouched nerves.

She wet her lips with a shiver. "You're getting greedy with my firsts."

"With you," he corrected, pressing harder, until one fingertip broached the tight ring of muscle.

Ford was greedy with her, because he wanted her. Her, not a fainting virgin or an obedient whore. So she buried her face against his neck and closed her eyes. "Take all of me."

"You have no idea." The words blew hot on her ear, sending a shiver rocketing through her. He held her captive—his hand on her back, his finger inside her—as he drove up into her, over and over, harder and harder.

And she realized she was going to come again.

Not easy this time. Not gentle. It was slow, pure friction and that primal jolt when his cock sank deep. And if she could have gotten a hand between them to rub her clit, she could have sent herself flying.

But she couldn't. She could only moan against his throat and let him take her there, let him lose them both in the slick slide of skin and the sound of him fucking up into her, until one final slam of his hips broke open the world.

She muffled a scream against his throat, and he gripped her hair and hauled her head back. "Let me hear it, Mia. Let me—"

She couldn't stop. She shook in his grip, moaning as her pussy clenched tight, giving him everything he wanted. Her relief, her pleasure, her shameless satisfaction.

He took it with a groan, his cock pulsing inside her as he set his teeth in her shoulder and followed her over the edge.

The world floated back to her in bits and pieces. His grip in her hair eased, and she nuzzled her face against his neck, still shivering with the tiny aftershocks. His hand settled at her back again, warm and strong, and her sleepy mind turned it into a symbol of everything Sector Four could be.

Strength. Tenderness. Holding her close without holding her down. That was the promise of Dallas O'Kane, of all the O'Kanes.

She was starting to believe it.

11

Mia was flying so high, she didn't see the danger until she crashed into it.

Into *him*.

Vaughn was waiting for her when she turned the corner from the baker. He sneered down at her, taking in her mussed hair and clothes wrinkled from the night on Ford's floor. "Mia."

Her thoughts skittered in a dozen directions, because it didn't seem real. Cold, meticulously dressed Vaughn didn't fit here in the rough edges of Sector Four. He didn't fit with the person she'd become, and for a horrifying moment that person slipped away, leaving a terrified, wounded girl.

He saw the fear in her. He had always been good at that—Vaughn didn't have the excuse of obliviousness to explain why he'd hurt her. He understood people and their emotions just fine. He simply didn't care about them.

He didn't care about her, and the knowledge made her lips numb as she swallowed hard. "I'm not going back with you."

He scoffed. "Yes, you are. Cerys is ready to collect her annual payment. I won't pay for something I no longer possess, and you know what that means."

It meant Cerys would come for her. Six years of training meant six years of patronage fees before Orchid House would consider its investment repaid—and Mia had barely managed one.

Cerys would come for her, and that was still preferable to taking one step closer to Vaughn. "So don't pay. You never wanted me in any case."

"You don't seem to understand." He moved, looming over her, his features set in anger. "I'll not be gossiped about because my whore left me."

She waited for the fear—for the terror—but something else bubbled up inside her. It filled her, surging higher as his hot breath fell across her forehead. He thought he could smack her into place with cruel words and physical intimidation, but he'd made the mistake of coming to Sector Four.

Her place was wherever the hell she wanted it to be.

Channeling Lex at her most cutting, Mia smiled. "It must be embarrassing, having everyone know you can't even pay a woman to tolerate you."

"Very funny." He grabbed her upper arm, his fingers biting painfully into her flesh. "I *should* hand you back to Cerys and get a replacement. Her house turns out better than you."

The alley they were standing in was narrow, empty. But they weren't far from the market. One scream would bring onlookers. Saying she worked for Dallas would turn gawkers into rescuers. Everyone would jump at the chance to rescue an O'Kane employee and secure Dallas's favor.

Maybe it wasn't her power, but she'd use it if she had to.

Clutching at that borrowed confidence, she ignored his grip on her arm and held Vaughn's gaze. No fear. No worry. Just bored amusement to match her borrowed smile. "You couldn't even handle me. One of Cerys's best students would eat you alive."

"A touching admission of your own shortcomings."

"If that's what you call them," she agreed easily. "All that training in business, accounting, and tech, *and* I could swallow a man's dick. You never deserved me."

Vaughn's lip curled. "Poor little Mia's developed some delusions of grandeur."

Her confidence cracked. Just a little. A fracture. But it was enough to let doubt creep in, and she jerked against his grip before she could stop herself. "So what if I have. I'm not your problem anymore. Send Cerys after me, I don't care."

Vaughn was a shark, and he smelled blood in the water. "You think someone's going to protect you if a sector leader comes for you, is that it?"

Ford would protect her, even if God himself came for her. After last night, she was sure of it. But she didn't want Ford tangled up in her past, didn't want to owe him her independence and spend the next night in his bed wondering if she'd traded one sort of patron for another.

But Ford wasn't the only person she could turn to. "Lex will. Maybe you've heard of her."

Vaughn snorted. "You're better off selling yourself

on the street than looking to imitate Alexa Parrino's fairy tale. A gallant, tattooed knight to buy you from Cerys? Please."

Mia doubted Dallas had ever paid a cent to Cerys, because Lex understood. She knew about choices and freedom, too.

This time she jerked hard enough to break free of his grip. "Then I'll sell myself on the street. You think that's a worse fate than being with you?"

He didn't grab her again. He shoved her against the wall, pinning her there with the bulk of his body. "I don't give a shit, Mia. But what's mine is mine."

The back of her head cracked into the wall, slamming her teeth together on the tip of her tongue. The bag slipped from her suddenly limp fingers. She tasted blood, tasted *fear*.

Vaughn would take her back to Sector Two. He wouldn't touch her—he'd never touch her, not with the corruption of Sector Four added to her many sins—but he'd whore her out to every trading partner he had. He'd do it out of spite, to show her her place, to punish her for wanting more.

He'd do all of it...but only if she let him.

He was still smirking down at her when she rammed her knee into his balls.

Mia had been gone too long just to pick up breakfast.

Ford rolled out of bed and dressed quickly, all the while telling himself he was being stupid. There were a dozen ways she could have been delayed—waiting for more coffee to brew or pastries to bake, a conversation, anything. And she'd be offended as hell when he showed up in the market like a possessive, crazy asshole.

He went anyway.

Ford was halfway across the street just outside the border of the O'Kane compound when the kid from the robbery skidded to a stop in front of him. His face still bore the bruises of Ford's smackdown, but there was nothing but eager concern in his eyes. "Your girl," he panted, jerking a finger toward the market. "Some slick dude in a suit—"

Ford's heart shot into his throat. Someone from Sector Two—one of Cerys's men, maybe even Mia's former patron himself.

He brushed past the kid and ran, ignoring the dull ache that sparked in his leg. He rounded the corner closest to Lou and Pam's coffee cart and saw Mia leaning against the wall, ignoring Pam as the older woman dabbed at her lip with a napkin.

She was bruised and bleeding but alive, all of her focus locked on Ike Armstrong as the cage fighter swung a meaty fist into a suited man's gut.

It had to be Vaughn. Ford rushed in, edging Ike out of the way as fury pounded in his head, blurring his vision. He snatched the man up by his jacket lapels and got in his face. "You think you're a big man, coming here?"

"Ford—" Mia started.

Vaughn cut her off with a cold, abrupt laugh. "I think I'm a man who doesn't care to waste money. She stole from me."

"Cry me a river." He jerked the man up, close to his face. "Did you do that to her lip?"

Instead of answering, Vaughn turned to Mia. "You idiot girl. You really did try to copy Lex, didn't you? Does he know how much he'll owe Cerys—?"

Ford slipped his fingers in the man's rumpled tie and twisted, cutting off his air while he counted to five.

Slowly. "Don't look at her—look at me. And answer the fucking question."

"He won't," Mia said quietly. "He's used to negotiating with the illegal farms. He's cruel and petty, but he's not easily intimidated."

Vaughn locked gazes with Ford—and in that moment, Ford knew he'd answer. Not out of fear, or respect, but just to make Mia wrong.

"Too late." Ford hauled back and punched him, a clean right hook to the jaw.

Vaughn staggered back, swaying violently. "She owes me for a year of soft living," he spat, eyes wild with hate. "I paid for a lady, and they sent me a whore."

He just didn't know when to shut his mouth, did he? Rage boiled up, hazing Ford's already blurry vision with red, and he jumped on Vaughn, driving him to the ground. He didn't realize he'd drawn back his fist until it connected with the man's nose, and then it happened again, and again.

And again.

"Ford!"

Hands locked around his arm. He tried to swing again, and Mia jerked back with a yelp of protest. "*Derek*, stop. He's not worth this."

Her words cut through the insensate fury, bringing the world around him into sharp relief. The blood on his aching hands, the pain jolting through his bad leg, the tension of his clenched teeth. And the man beneath him, who deserved every ounce of the ass-whipping and more.

But Mia had asked him to stop. So he heaved a breath, sat back on his heels, his leg screaming, and looked up at the man standing behind her. "Get him the hell out of here, Ike. Dump him somewhere near the wall, and he can find his way back home."

Ike Armstrong grunted, hoisted Vaughn's limp body over one broad shoulder, and headed for the end of the street. The gawking crowd parted in front of him, took one look at Ford, and scattered. Pam glanced between him and Mia, muttered something about a first aid kit, and hurried after them.

"It's okay." Mia crouched in front of him and slid a hand over his. "That fighter showed up so fast, Vaughn barely had a chance to touch me. And I kneed him right in his tiny dick."

She moved fast, edgy like a nervous bird, and the sheer apprehension in her voice kicked Ford's anger a notch higher. "Bullshit," he said slowly. Clearly. "You know whatever he said to you was bullshit, right?"

"I know." But she wouldn't look at him, wouldn't meet his eyes. "It doesn't make me any less of a fool for misjudging his pride."

Pride hadn't brought him here, arrogance had. The soul-deep conviction that it was his right to waltz into another territory to take back what was his.

Fuck that.

Ford rose. "I should have killed him."

"No." Mia reached for her battered bag of pastries before straightening. "I have to stop running. I can deal with Cerys, but it will cost me more if she has to cover up a dead patron."

"Maybe, if he stayed in his own damn sector. But he came to *ours*, starting trouble. He deserves whatever he gets."

The bag crinkled as her fingers clenched tight, and even that couldn't hide her trembling hands. "I'm sorry."

He wanted to reach for her, but with his own hands still shaking—not to mention bloody—it seemed wrong, somehow. "Sorry for what? Walking through the market? Minding your own goddamn business?"

"For bringing trouble. For stopping you from kill-ing him. I don't know if..." She trailed off, pressing her fingertips to her bruised lip. "Was it political? Will you be in trouble for letting him go?"

It wouldn't go well for Vaughn if he squawked about it. Even in Two, few would sympathize with him for venturing into another sector and getting his ass kicked. "If Cerys didn't know where you were before, she will now."

Mia nodded jerkily before finally meeting his eyes. "What Vaughn said *was* bullshit. What's between us has nothing to do with Cerys. I don't want you to give her anything."

He was being a jerk, making her feel worse. Ford sighed and took her in his arms. "Are you all right?"

"I think so." At least she relaxed into him, burying her face against his throat as her arms went around him. "People protected me. Strangers. Because of you."

His arms locked around her—too tight, but he couldn't seem to ease his hold. "I should have been here."

"You didn't have to be." She tilted her head back and smiled, even though her split lip made her wince. "Maybe you can't understand, but that matters. Even if the power isn't mine, even if he only stepped in to get attention from Dallas—it's as close to independent as I've ever been."

A heartbreaking admission. Ford dropped a care-ful kiss to her forehead. "Come on, let's get back. You might want to talk to Lex."

She winced again—and hid her face against his shirt with a groan. "She's going to lecture me. She wouldn't have stopped you."

No, she wouldn't have. Lex got a lot of things when

it came to the harsh realities of day-to-day existence—about life in the sectors, about survival and even running away.

And, maybe more than anything else, she understood about protecting people you cared about and taking action when it was warranted.

She would understand what Ford had to do.

12

Ford insisted on first aid, a bath, and breakfast in that order. By the time Mia took a seat in Dallas and Lex's office, she was wishing she'd skipped that last one. Her cinnamon rolls and coffee formed a tight knot in her stomach as she faced Lex across the massive wooden desk.

Lex eyed her mildly. "It's catching up with you, huh?"

Mia didn't know if Lex was talking about the past or that morning, but her answer was the same either way. "Yes."

"Leaving feels like such a final thing, and then you find out it's only the first step." She sighed. "Sucker punch."

"I didn't think he'd come after me," she admitted, and because Lex would understand, she let her frustration creep into her voice. "I *know* better. Of course he came after me. It was never about whether or not he valued me. I let him hurt me, and then I let that pain make me stupid."

Lex waved that away. "Vaughn's not your problem now. He comes here again, he gets his ass kicked—or worse. But if Cerys shows up..."

"Five years." Even saying it out loud made Mia twist her fingers together. One year of patron fees for an Orchid could support a poor family in the sectors eighteen months or more. Even the new, ridiculously extravagant weekly salary Ford had insisted on giving her would barely chip away at how much she'd owe. "She'll demand it all, won't she?"

"At the very least." Lex rolled her eyes. "And then she'll find a way to pad the amount, because that's the kind of mercenary bitch she is."

Mia didn't doubt it. Every house in Sector Two fed its girls on the fantasy of accomplished initiates who had served out the necessary years to repay their training before going on to become fabulously wealthy. After all, a girl who made it that far received a quarter of her patronage fee—minus expenses—every year until she retired.

Minus expenses. Mia had no doubt that Cerys could pull out a record of every time she'd visited the spa during her year with Vaughn. The costs would be tallied with damning results. A hundred dollars for a bar of soap. Two hundred for a manicure. Fifty dollars for a glass of lemonade.

Any woman who'd ever retired wealthy in Sector Two had been allowed to do so, because someone had to keep the dream alive.

"I can't tell Ford," Mia said quietly. "He'll try to pay it. Or he'll give me another ridiculous raise."

"Mmm. And I'd lend it to you, but if I were you? It'd feel a little too much like trading one owner for another."

The anxiety twisting her guts into knots tightened into an agony of guilt, because Lex had given her so much already, and it wasn't fair to feel wary. But Lex didn't look upset. She looked like she understood, and all of that tension unraveled so fast, Mia slumped back in her chair.

"I know you wouldn't mean it like that," she said, meeting Lex's eyes. "But that's what we were trained to appreciate, isn't it? The balance of power."

"Without a doubt." Lex lifted one eyebrow. "I do know one person who has that kind of money who might be willing to help out *and* wouldn't make your new life awkward."

"An O'Kane?"

"Newly minted," Lex confirmed. "You know Jade, right?"

A question with layers. Jade was the one who had gotten Mia the job with the O'Kanes, so Lex must know they were acquainted. But asking gave Mia a graceful exit, a way to demure without rejecting an offer. All she had to say was *not very well* and the conversation would move on.

"I know her," she said instead. "She helped me when I first came to Sector Four. Bought me some clothes and stayed with me while I visited the doctor. But this is so much more to ask..."

"It is," Lex agreed. "But consider that it might not just be something you need. It might be something Jade needs, too."

Mia could see that. Cerys had betrayed Jade on a fundamental level, shattering the one bond of trust that supported the fragile illusion of Sector Two. *We're in this together* was the lie they told with smiles and grand promises, but Jade was the reality. She'd climbed higher than any other woman in Two, and all Cerys had cared about was using her hard, using her up.

Which answered *why*, but not *how*. "If she's willing, I'd be grateful. But are you sure she can afford it?"

Lex chuckled. "Yeah, I'm sure."

No details, but Mia supposed she should have expected that Lex wouldn't share secrets. If things went well, someday Mia might know Jade well enough to ask how she'd escaped from Sector Two with that kind of wealth. For now she'd just be grateful. "I don't want to wait for Cerys to come after me. I need this to be over."

"Because you can't have it hanging over your head, or because Ford won't let it be? Because I can make him, you know."

"It wouldn't help, because I've already fucked him." The words spilled out, blunt and defensive, and Mia didn't let them hang there, shaming her. She didn't retreat. "And I want to do it again, and I can't. Not like this."

Lex regarded her thoughtfully. "Fair enough. It's hard to move forward when the past is sitting on your shoulders, after all."

Fair enough. No recriminations, no disapproval. Mia rubbed her palms against her legs as if she could scrub away the feeling that she deserved it. "I know I'm being reckless. He's still an O'Kane, and I'm not. And I work for him. He still has all of the power."

"With one difference." Lex leaned back in her chair and swiveled it gently, left to right. "If you said no, Ford would respect that, and so would we."

Ford would respect her *no*. If she'd had any doubts about that, she never would have touched him to begin with. But that wouldn't make him eager to sit across a desk from her day after day if things went wrong.

It all came down to trust and if the way he made her feel was worth the risk. It was something she'd have to figure out soon.

As soon as she'd shaken free of the past.

Jasper McCray was nothing like Mia had imagined.

Dallas's second-in-command was a large, serious man who didn't need to rely on subtle symbols of power to look intimidating. His size and strength alone conveyed a warning. His full beard, endless tattoos, and battered leather vest conveyed something else. Surrounded by the clean-shaven, carefully tailored men of Sector Two, Jas looked like the only man who wasn't trying too hard.

She'd expected all of that. He was the dangerous criminal who'd lured a councilman's daughter into an illicit affair, after all. No man overly worried about reprisals would have taken up with Noelle Cunningham. But the gentleness under all that raw danger was a seductive flame in the middle of a frozen winter. Mia could see why a terrified city girl had flung herself at this man and held on for dear life.

No one within the circle of Jasper McCray's protection had to worry about mundane threats, and having him at her back as they waited for Cerys was the only thing keeping Mia's nerves from blooming into outright panic.

"You're gonna be okay," he said gruffly. "It's a simple transaction. We'll be out of here in no time."

Mia tried for a smile. It tugged at her barely healed lip, and she hated that. It would have been smarter to wait a day, until med-gel and time had given her a chance to face Cerys with all her masks in place.

It would be harder like this, with all of her vulnerabilities on display. But it would be over. "Thank you for coming with me."

"Hey, no problem. Whatever you need."

The door in front of them opened, and Mia barely kept from reaching for Jasper's hand. But it wasn't Cerys. Instead, a familiar blonde stepped out of Cerys's office.

Susi had been a friend. A sister. Mia's heart thumped hard when the other woman caught sight of her. Susi's eyes widened. Relief flickered across her face, and pleasure, and Mia opened her mouth to greet her—

Too late. Susi's gaze had jumped to Jas. To his wrists, and the O'Kane tattoos curled around them, as legendary as Dallas O'Kane himself. The blood drained from Susi's face. Fear filled her big blue eyes.

A few months ago, Mia might have had the same reaction. She'd been trained as surely as Susi, taught to fear Sector Four, to fear the O'Kanes and everything they stood for. Cerys took few chances now, grinding the fear deep into every girl who might look at her and look at Lex and see salvation.

Susi had never had a patron. She'd never seen the truth beneath the pretty lies, or had any reason to doubt that the O'Kanes were the real monsters.

Susi still believed in the dream.

With a last, regretful look at Mia, she caught up her robes and hurried away, leaving Mia cold and sad and—for one moment—totally alone.

Jasper swore softly, the sound almost drowned out by the mellifluous chime that filled the room.

Mia was on her feet before she realized she had moved, and she hated it. Hated that there were instincts buried so deep she might not realize they were there until Cerys jerked the leash. She might spend months digging them out, one by one. She might spend years.

But she'd do it. All she had to do was walk into that office and buy her freedom.

Squaring her shoulders, Mia tightened her grip on the envelope holding a fortune in credits and strode into Cerys's domain for the last time.

The woman sat behind her wide desk, impeccably dressed, every lock of hair arranged artfully around her shoulders. "Mia. It's good to see you."

The chair set on the opposite side of the desk was shorter than Cerys's. Not so much the average person would notice, but sitting in it would make her feel small. She couldn't have this conversation with Cerys looming over her.

So she remained standing, consciously relaxing her hands until the envelope rested lightly between her fingers. No outward show of anxiety. No unnecessary signs of weakness. No polite chit-chat before getting to the point. "You know I'm here to pay off my training debt. I calculated my expenses. I have the credits."

Cerys blinked at her before reaching for the slender cigarette already burning on her desk. She lifted its slim black holder to her lips and paused. "I'm listening."

"Vaughn wasn't concerned with my safety." She let an edge creep into her voice. "If you care about protecting your girls, even a little, you won't trust him with another Orchid."

"I've spoken with him. He has no interest in taking on responsibility for another Orchid." One corner of Cerys's perfectly painted mouth tipped up. "You saw to that. I referred him to Rose House."

An empty victory, diverting Vaughn's cruelty from women trained to handle it to women taught to endure it. Jade had always been the exception that proved the rule when it came to Rose House—an initiate who could handle *and* endure. Too many of the other girls would simply submit in truth, letting Vaughn chip away at their sense of self-worth until they broke under the pain.

Mia should have let Ford kill the bastard.

The rage creeping under her skin made it harder to stay calm. "How much? How much so I can walk away?"

Cerys sighed. "Are you certain you want to?"

"What possible alternative could you offer?"

"You could come back. Stay, and help train the girls."

An offer that should have turned her stomach, but Cerys was clever. Her traps came in layers, the kind you baited yourself. *Train* the girls could so easily become *warn* the girls, and for one reckless moment, Mia considered it. She could stay here, fomenting quiet, subversive rebellion. She could start more whispers, chip away at the dream Cerys was peddling. Feed the dream Lex represented.

Maybe that's what Jade had been planning before Cerys agreed to start drugging her.

She held up the envelope. "I'm certain. Tell me how much you want."

The woman's dark gaze dropped to the heavy envelope, but she only sat back with a mild shrug. "Nothing. You're free to go."

Nothing in life was that easy. Mia studied Cerys's face, struggling to find the trap, but she couldn't even find the hint of triumph that would mean it had already snapped shut around her. The only possibility that made any sense was that this was a snub, a way of Cerys reinforcing one last time how very little Mia was worth...

The woman watching her with that easy, unbothered gaze hadn't seized control of a sector by making petty, financially stupid decisions out of spite. She might let Mia walk away, but it wouldn't be freedom. "I don't want to go until my debt is clear."

"I forgive it."

"I don't believe you."

"And why not?"

Because Cerys didn't forgive debts, unless someone else—

Her stomach flipped. The envelope almost slipped through her fingers, and she tightened them until the edges crumpled in. "Who? Who paid you?"

Cerys had turned her attention back to flipping through the neat stack of papers on her desk, and she didn't look up as she answered. "Who else? Your new patron."

13

The door to his office flung open and crashed against the wall so hard that Ford almost dropped his tablet.

Mia stepped through and slammed it shut even harder.

"How could you?" She stalked toward his desk, fury in every line of her body but her face—her eyes were a gut punch of pain and betrayal, even as she slapped her hands against his desk. "I told you to *leave it alone.*"

Oh, shit. "Because I had the money, Mia. You can pay me back. Or not, I don't really care. The important thing is that Cerys is out of your life for good."

"Oh, is that the important thing?" She leaned over the desk, until her face hovered so close her vicious whisper was almost a caress. "If my new patron thinks that's the most important thing, who am I to disagree? Thank you, sir."

A chill raced up his spine, and he rose. "Jesus Christ, *patron*? Don't be ridiculous."

"You bought me, Ford." She shoved away from the desk and paced, stripping off her jacket with abrupt, angry movements. "You handed the woman who sold me to Vaughn a stack of cash, and you made the decision without me."

He would have apologized in the face of her anger—the last thing he'd meant to do was upset her—but framing the situation in such tawdry terms pissed him off, too. "What decision? You owed Cerys money, now you don't."

"No, now I owe you money." She pivoted back to glare at him. "How many kinds of power do you need over me? You're an O'Kane. You're my boss. Every scrap of power and safety I have is borrowed from you, and now my freedom is, too."

What was his alternative? To watch her glancing back over her shoulder every time a stranger walked by, just in case it was one of Cerys's men? To see her scramble to save enough money to pay the debt, knowing full well she never could?

Fuck that. Ford crossed his arms over his chest. "I'd do it again."

Her eyebrows swept up. "That's your response to seeing how much it hurt me? *I'd do it again?* And I'm supposed to believe you don't want control over my life?"

"I'd do it again because you're being silly," he countered. "You let all this shit get in your head, and now you're shoving it off on me. I was helping you, that's all."

"Like I was trying to *help* you on my first day by

acting like you couldn't walk across the room to file some papers on your own?"

Things were going wrong, spinning out of control. All she needed was to be placated, for him to apologize, and he opened his mouth, but the words wouldn't come. Frustrated, he ground out a curse and ran his hands through his hair. "This is stupid, Mia. It's a stupid argument."

She clutched her coat against her chest, her posture rigid. Defensive. "Maybe it's stupid that you walk all over this damn sector without your cane. And that you hide up here, licking your wounds, when you have a whole family out there who loves you whether your leg works or not. Or that you're so desperate to hide your weakness you can't see how strong you are. Maybe all of those things are stupid, but they're not stupid to me. Because they matter to you."

That brought him up short and stabbed pain through the center of his chest. Ford dropped his hands by his sides. "I just wanted you to be safe, and now you are."

"I hope so." Mia slipped a hand into her jacket pocket and pulled out an envelope. It clicked with the sound of credit sticks bumping together when she set it on his desk. "This should cover what you paid. If I still have a job, I'd like the rest of the day off."

"If you still—" He bit his tongue to cut off the words. "Thanks a lot, Mia."

She flinched and turned for the door. "Making me feel guilty for standing up for myself doesn't make you right. It makes you like him."

"And you feeling like a whore doesn't mean I treated you like one." The pain in his chest deepened into an ache that throbbed through him. "You didn't even ask me why I went to Cerys. You just came in here, throwing around ugly words, thinking shit around here is exactly like it was back home in Two. So yeah, one of us is exactly like Vaughn. But it isn't me."

Her steps faltered, but she didn't look back. Just opened the door, and closed it carefully behind her.

Go after her. Ford wrapped both hands around the edge of his desk to keep from obeying the silent command screaming through him. Why should he, when she was the one who hadn't even afforded him a chance to explain before tearing into him? Before comparing him to the bastard who'd treated her like shit.

No. He relaxed his fingers, sat down, and stared unseeingly at the papers on his desk. If she thought so little of him, so be it. She could run, but he *wasn't* like Vaughn.

He wouldn't chase her.

It wasn't a long walk from Ford's office to the rooms Nessa had so generously offered to share. Down the steps at the back of the Broken Circle, across an empty parking lot and what might have been a street before the O'Kanes had commandeered four city blocks to build their sprawling home.

Most of the O'Kanes seemed to live in a large building on the far side of the compound, but Nessa was like Ford. She'd claimed space close to where she worked, which meant that getting there meant walking through the warehouse where the O'Kanes made their whiskey.

It meant walking by O'Kanes, Ford's brothers, men who glanced at her before looking away, because they didn't know yet. They didn't know that she was hysterical, or ungrateful, or whatever Ford would say when he complained about how crazy his goddamn assistant was.

If she even had her job anymore.

But she could handle the men. Nessa was the final straw, popping out of her office as Mia reached the stairs to the second floor. Nessa didn't glance at her and go about her business. She took one look at Mia's expression and swore. "Oh hell, what the fuck happened?"

So much defensive anger. It would vanish when the truth came out, because Nessa had ink wrapped around her wrists, too. She was an O'Kane, and Ford was family.

Mia was just a broken girl foolish enough to think freedom was real.

Her self-control crumpled. The tears that had been stinging at the back of her eyes overflowed, and she couldn't make them stop. Not when Nessa wrapped slender arms around her in a bruising hug, not when the other woman dragged her back into her office and down onto a couch, still holding on to her like Mia deserved comfort, deserved friendship.

That only made her cry harder.

"Jas said something was up." Lex hovered in the doorway, her shoulders tense. "Ford?"

"Probably, the asshole," Nessa grumbled, and the fact that she was talking about her like she wasn't even there was what let Mia seize control of her traitorous body.

"It's not—" Her voice cracked, and she eased from Nessa's grip and scrubbed her hands over her face. God, she couldn't face Lex like this. A wreck, every defense laid to waste, sobbing like a first-week initiate who still got homesick. "I'm okay. I'm sorry."

Lex knelt in front of the couch and peered up at Mia for a few moments before sighing. "Oh, shit. He didn't."

Hope flared, and it hurt. She hadn't realized how cast adrift she'd felt until she looked into Lex's face and saw comprehension. The world wobbled, and she reached for Lex, literally and metaphorically, clutching Lex's hands as she asked the question that could break her. "Am I overreacting?"

"I don't know, honey. Did you tell him he was being a presumptive ass?"

Mia closed her eyes with a pained laugh. "I probably said worse."

A pause. "How much worse?"

There was no point in hiding the truth, so she told Lex everything. What Cerys had said, what *she'd* said, sparing herself not at all...

And Ford's words. Even the ones that had cut the deepest because they seemed reasonable. Felt true. The ones that kept bleeding, because they echoed Vaughn's. Not in tone, but in meaning. *Poor, delusional Mia, thinking she has value. Thinking she can be free.*

Wasn't that what Ford had said, with actions if not words? He'd been saying it over and over since the start, and she'd let him. First the heater. Then the jacket. And the raise. Maybe she was the one sending mixed signals, letting him help her until her pride snapped.

And he meant well. God, she knew he did. But did it matter if he meant well, when every gift was a reminder that she needed someone in her life who meant well, who bridged the gap between her abilities and her ambitions?

So she told Lex everything. And when she ran out of words, she fell silent, staring at their joined hands, unable to look down into the face of a woman whose abilities so outstripped Mia's own that no ambition was out of reach.

"Motherfucker." Lex squinted as she pulled one hand free and rubbed the center of her forehead as if it ached. "He should *not* have done that, Mia—any of it. He had no right, and I'm sorry."

It was like standing across from Cerys again, hearing the words *You're free to go*. Too good to be true. "I lost my temper. I was mean."

"Hell yeah, you were. I'm not saying you acted like a peach, either."

"I knew how to hurt him," Mia agreed. "I think I wanted to. I wanted him to hurt me back."

"Makes it all easier, huh?" Lex rose before sliding onto the couch beside her. "You both got upset. It happens. What really matters is what you do now."

She said it like there were a million options. "I gave him the money I borrowed from Jade. I had to." And now she'd have to spend the next fifteen years working to pay off that debt.

Lex waved a hand. "Not what you do about the money. About Ford."

Mia dropped her gaze to the hand holding hers. To the ink etched over Lex's slender wrist. "I don't know. Listening to me when I say *no* isn't just about sex."

"No, it's not," she agreed.

"Did I do something wrong?"

"Wrong? Maybe." Lex slipped her fingers into Mia's hair and leaned her head against hers. "You let Cerys get in here and fuck you up. We've all done that. Were you wrong to be angry with Ford? No."

Mia took a deep breath and held it until her lungs burned. Then she let it out, slowly, and allowed the pain and hurt to slip away with it. "This is what Cerys wanted. Me, furious and hurt and desperate enough to take what she offered."

"And to make you think that things here couldn't be different. Better."

"Promise me they can be," she whispered, closing her eyes. "You know where I've been. What I am. Just tell me there's hope."

"It's definitely different," Lex answered. "How much better it can be depends on what you do, and what you want."

What do you want?

Lex had to know how overwhelming that question was. *Want* was an impulse, something she indulged on a whim. She wanted cinnamon rolls or a hot bath or Ford's hands on her body—stolen moments of seized opportunity.

Now she needed to make it more. She needed to dream. "If I figure it out, will you help me get there?"

"Of course I will." Lex's arm dropped to her shoulder for a quick squeeze. "It's what I do."

Work was impossible. Ford kept staring at the same figures, watching them swim together in an incomprehensible haze of numbers, until he finally gave up and reached for the bottle of whiskey in his desk drawer.

His hand had just closed around the bottle when a sharp rap rattled the door. Only one, and then the door pushed open and Dallas O'Kane was staring at him, eyes dark, face impassive. "Ford."

Terrific. Now, on top of the swirling confusion and pain, he'd have to explain himself like a little boy. "Come in, Dallas."

Dallas kicked the door shut and sank into a chair. "Guess it's not going to come as a surprise that you've got some of the ladies riled up."

No, the women would be circling the wagons, protecting Mia no matter what. "Surprise? Not really."

"Yeah, someone had to sit on Nessa to keep her from coming over here to crawl halfway up your ass." Dallas draped his arms across his chest and studied Ford. "The good news? Lex hasn't tried to stab you yet, so you've got that going for you."

"Maybe she just hasn't gotten around to it." Ford met his boss's gaze squarely. "Or she sent you to do it for her."

"Lex doesn't send a man to do her stabbing for her." Dallas exhaled and shook his head. "Relax, man. Yeah, you fucked up. Yeah, the girls circled the wagons. That's what they do. You know why?"

There was only one answer. "Because every single one of them knows what it's like to have some jackass man try to control their lives?"

"Pretty much. I'm sure plenty of those jackasses have had great intentions, too. Doesn't really matter when you're stepping all over someone's pride."

Pride. After her life in Sector Two, it had been so important to Mia, and he'd chipped away at it every day. The coat, the heater, the payment to Cerys—a never-ending cascade of reminders that, even here, her life wasn't her own.

He pulled the bottle out of the drawer and cracked it open. "You want one, Dallas?"

"Sure." Dallas watched him pour two drinks but didn't reach out to take the glass. "The only jackass man who gets to control Mia's life right now is me. And before I tell you what's going to happen, I'll say this. Part of this is on me. I should have come down harder on you about drawing some damn lines, at least until she was free of Cerys's sick shit."

"And I should have considered what it would be

like to come from a situation like that...and have to deal with me."

"Fuck yeah, you should have." Dallas swept up the whiskey and took a sip. When he eyed Ford over the edge of the glass, all of the warmth had left his eyes. The leader of Sector Four was staring at him now, hard and unyielding. "You contacted another sector leader behind my back, Ford."

"For personal business."

"None of us can afford to have personal business with other sector leaders. Especially with Cerys. Shit is sincerely unsettled right now, and I need a heads-up if anything—and I mean *anything*—might tip us off balance."

"Fair enough." Ford drained his glass and began refilling it. "I asked Cerys how much Mia owed her, then I wired her more credits than most people see in ten years."

"And then you let that girl go over there, oblivious, so Cerys could spin her circles."

He hadn't had a chance to tell Mia, because he wanted it done before approaching her. *So she wouldn't be able to say no, right?* "She could have asked me what it meant. Why I did it."

"She knows why you did it. In her gut, she knows, or she wouldn't have come back. Or she only would have come back long enough to steal all your files and bring them to Cerys." Dallas slammed back the rest of his shot and relaxed back in his chair. "What do you want more? To be right, or to make things right?"

Ford almost snorted whiskey out of his nose. "Be right? That fucking ship has sailed, O'Kane. Best I can hope for now is for Mia not to hate me."

"If she keeps working for you, yeah." Dallas pinned him with a look. "Which is why, starting tomorrow, she's working for me."

It hurt more than everything else combined. Ford tightened his fingers around the neck of the bottle as he fought a wince. "Is that how it is?"

"You're still not getting it." Dallas thumped the glass against the desk. "Power, Derek. You're an O'Kane, you're rich, you've got all the advantages over her. So I'm doing what I can to level the field. I'm not slapping you down. I'm giving you a chance."

A chance—to be someone Mia could come to without reservation, without worrying about whether she needed to fight him on every little thing just to maintain her own equilibrium. If he wasn't her boss, she could embrace the submission she'd claimed to want instead of worrying that doing so meant giving in. Giving up.

Ford met Dallas's gaze across the desk. "Have you talked to her about it yet?"

"It's a done deal. I'm setting her loose with Noelle in the tech storage room tomorrow. We'll see what she's capable of."

"A lot." Something Ford should have told her.

"Yeah?" Dallas seemed to consider that as he leaned in to grab the whiskey. "You want to give her something she needs?"

"Anything."

Dallas refilled his glass before spinning the bottle in his hand to rub a thumb over the label—over their logo. His logo. "She's not working for you anymore. That doesn't mean she can't work with you. Show her what we can offer. Show *me* what *she* can offer. I could have Ace give her ink tomorrow, but it would be just as damn empty as you paying off Cerys. Help her earn her ink, and then she'll have the kind of power no one can take away."

The kind the other women had, the kind Lex had

been fighting for since day one. "Where do I start?"

"In my experience? *I'm sorry*. And sometimes presents. Lex likes knives." Dallas grinned and lifted his glass. "I know I'm forgiven if she only cuts me a little."

There was only one thing he could think of to give Mia, and it would be the weirdest goddamn gift ever.

Which was why it just might work.

14

By the second day of her new job, Mia understood how Ford had been so cavalier about tossing expensive tech at her.

Dallas O'Kane had more. *Lots* more.

"This was all a jumble when I showed up," Noelle had confessed yesterday morning, waving to shelf after shelf of neatly organized and labeled boxes. "It's been my side project."

It needed to be more than a side project, Mia could see that at once. Dallas's aversion to technology was almost understandable—he was old enough to have been born just after the Flares, which meant his earliest memories must have been the darkness that followed. Data winking out of existence as circuits fried and overloaded, a world in chaos because paper records had long ago been a thing of the past...

So she understood why he clung to something tangible, something that couldn't simply vanish. Hard copy had its uses...as a backup.

Mia could make that work. With the tech in this room, she could make damn near anything work. She should have been vibrating with excitement, with the possibilities of wrapping her brain around the entire O'Kane operation and finding all the ways to automate the process, to smooth off the inefficient edges.

Her chest felt hollow. Her neck and shoulders ached. She kept catching herself tensing against a blow that wasn't coming—not physically, anyway. She'd been too cowardly to face Ford, but she was only delaying the inevitable. He was an O'Kane. She wouldn't be able to avoid him forever.

Even knowing that, she still wasn't ready when he appeared. Maybe if she'd known, she could have braced herself for the moment, or found the focus to build a polite mask. But she stepped out from between two shelves and there he was, as dangerously handsome as ever, watching her.

Waiting.

But not for long. He shoved his hands into his pockets and nodded to her. "Mia."

She needed to cling to her mask, to act calm and reserved as she carried the box of supplies to the desk she'd already started to think of as hers. But that mask felt wrong with him still. Fakeness felt wrong. What was the point of giving up everything for independence if you were still trapped in a cage?

She dropped the box to the desk with a soft *thud* and met his gaze. "I should have come to talk to you. I'm sorry."

He shook his head. "I didn't mean to interrupt your work."

"You're not." She fixed her gaze on his cheek, because it was easier than looking into his eyes. If they went all soft and warm, her resolve would waver. And he'd have so many rationalizations, so many reasons he'd meant well... "I'll still help you with your office, whenever you need me. If you need me, I mean."

The corner of his mouth wrinkled up in a half-smile. "Nah, I think Dallas has decided I'm better off working alone. Especially since you made such an amazing program already. It'll help a lot."

No, his cheek wasn't safe, not when it was that close to his mouth. She tore her gaze away and stared down. "I'm sorry I compared you to Vaughn. That was unfair. I hate what you did, but I know you were trying to help, and that's the one thing Vaughn was never trying to do."

Ford snorted. "You were right. There was *one thing* you needed from me, and I couldn't get it done. I'm sorry."

Two simple words, and they ripped the ground out from under her.

Surprise finally drove her to meet his eyes, and part of her still expected insincerity. Mockery. Powerful men didn't apologize. Especially not to ungrateful girls who'd spurned their gifts, shrieked at them in a rage, and stormed out of their lives. But Ford was watching her like he meant it, like he *believed* it, and when her lips parted, nothing came out.

"So, yeah." He pulled a slip of paper from his pocket and held it out. "Here. You can talk terms with Dallas. It's his show now."

Mia took the paper and stared at it until the words swam into focus.

And then she kept staring.

Ford had handed her a bill. Everything he'd given

her was listed in a neat row, along with the cost in credits. And, for one heartbreaking moment, it felt like a punishment. She'd walked away from him, and he'd come after her, wanting to recoup his investment. Just like Cerys.

But this bill was different. She'd watched Trix buy the coat, and Ford had fudged the numbers, underestimating the cost. Not enough to turn this into a patronizing joke, but enough to blunt the edge of the final total. He'd done it with everything on the list, undoubtedly fighting the urge to keep trimming, to take away the burden instead of adding to it.

Because greed was in Cerys's nature, but it wasn't in his. Not like this.

He hadn't just handed her a bill. He'd handed her a clean slate.

The edge of the paper crinkled under her fingers, and she realized her hand was shaking. She set it down on the desk and smoothed out the creases. "Did Lex tell you to do this?"

He grimaced. "Lex isn't exactly speaking to me at the moment."

"Because of me?"

"Because I was thoughtless," he countered quietly. "Because I would have known better if I'd stopped to think about something besides myself."

It was a statement as profound as anything Lex had said, because it made her reassurances more than comforting words. Ford had crossed a line. Lex believed it. Dallas believed it.

Ford believed it.

Her clean slate stretched out in front of her. An empty canvas, and she could fill it with anything she was brave enough to reach for. She could fill her life with him.

Gathering her courage and her pride, she stroked the edge of the bill. "Can I ask a favor?"

"Anything." His calm demeanor cracked, just a little, regret and a shred of hope splashed across his features. "I'd still do anything, Mia."

She swept up the paper and took one step—figurative and literal—toward meeting him in the middle. Because having the power to say *no* made *yes* so much easier. "Could you help me pay this?"

"Help you?" he echoed.

"You can't pay back Jade," she said, as hope and nerves danced dizzily in her stomach. "I bought my life back, and I need to pay the debt. That's the only way it'll ever feel real. But the little things...maybe too much pride is as dangerous as none."

He nodded, his throat working as he swallowed. "I can do that, buttercup."

"You don't have to be afraid to let me choose, Derek." The paper fluttered between them as she held it out. "Because Dallas is wrong. You're not better off alone. I choose you."

He brushed past her outstretched hand, wrapped one strong arm around her waist, and dragged her to him.

Mia let everything go. The bill, her terror, a lifetime of holding back. She rose up on her toes and buried her fingers in his hair, drawing so close her lips almost touched his. "It's better this way. You know why?"

His answering rumble vibrated against her lips. "Why?"

Because all of the games they'd both been dancing around could be hotter and darker and rawer, because they would only be as real as she let them be. "For one thing, now you can tell me to pull up my skirt and bend over your desk, and I might do it."

He licked her lower lip as his hand slid down to her ass, clutching her firmly against him. "You would have anyway, just to find out what happened."

"Maybe," she admitted, since it was true. The thought had always heated her blood, and now she could let it. Freedom and responsibility in her life, freedom *from* responsibility in his bed—it was the opposite of everything Sector Two stood for, and it was hers for the taking.

So she took it. Parted her lips and claimed him, muffling his groan as her tongue slid over his. Deeper and rougher than ever before, especially when he clutched the back of her head and tilted his mouth to hers.

Taking, because the line had been there for him, too. Now the only lines left were the ones they drew together.

Not that she was drawing many now. The harder he kissed her, the more eagerly her body reacted. She was flushed already, breathless and melting, and if he jerked up her borrowed skirt and snuck his fingers between her thighs, he'd know just how hot she was.

But he didn't lift her skirt. He lifted *her*, turned, and settled her on one of the wide steel desks along the wall. Mia edged her knees apart, making room for his hips between her thighs. Over his shoulder she could see the wide-open door and the hallway beyond.

It wasn't exactly fucking up against the cage during fight night, but the possibility of being caught zipped through her, bringing with it a fresh surge of exhilaration as she reached for his shirt. He batted her hands aside, but only long enough to tear open the buttons on her shirt.

He cupped her breasts through the lace of her bra and bent his head to them with a groan—one she echoed when his mouth opened over one nipple. The flimsy fabric wasn't enough to shield her from heat that only grew more intense when he worked the edge down and his mouth met flesh.

Mia arched her spine, whimpering when her shoulders slammed against the wall. Unyielding concrete at her back, unyielding man in front of her. She had been totally naked and felt less debauched than she did like this, almost entirely clothed.

Then his hands slipped under her skirt.

"Belt," he rumbled against her skin.

"What?" Those big, wonderful fingers were sliding up the insides of her thighs, and this time he wouldn't go easy with them. Just a few more inches and he'd realize how wet her panties were, how much she wanted this moment—

His fingers bit into her thighs, and he nipped at her chin—hard. "Unbuckle my belt, Mia. Now."

Her hands trembled. She had to take a steadying breath and slow her movements, guiding the supple leather free of the silver buckle. "What else? Tell me."

His rasping laugh shivered up her spine. "Get your fucking hands on my dick, buttercup."

Oh God, *yes*.

She fumbled with his fly and shoved aside his underwear, and she didn't care if Noelle came back from lunch and caught her jerking Ford off. It was probably only a matter of time until she came back and found Jas bending Noelle over a table, because squeezing every possible drop of joy out of every spare moment seemed to be what the O'Kanes were all about.

There was so much pleasure in this. In the heat of his cock under her fingers, in the way her touch made him groan and arch up against her hands. She caught his gaze and licked her palm before wrapping it around him, and he answered by edging his fingers into her panties and thrusting them into her.

Maybe she was getting used to having him inside her body, because she barely registered the discomfort. His fingers were still broad and long, but she was wet and a hundred years past ready, straining to spread her knees wider as she stroked him. "Don't make me wait. Please."

"Not another second," he promised roughly. He tore at her panties, the delicate lace yielding beneath his hand as he dragged her with the other to the edge of the desk. "Do it. Put me inside you."

There was something deliciously lewd about the words, about obeying them. She gripped his shaft and teased herself with the broad head, slicking it over her clit with a gasp. But it wasn't enough. It wouldn't be enough until he was buried deep, so she guided him into place.

And waited.

It killed her not to lift her hips, not to wrap her legs around him and drag him forward. He hovered there, just barely inside her, and she shivered and stared up into his eyes. "When we're like this? I'll take anything you want to give me."

Ford looked down at her, his gaze fixed on her lips. "Do you need it, Mia?"

A question with a dozen meanings. Did she need his cock, did she need the sweet freedom of sexual submission, did she need this relationship and whatever it could be, did she need *him*?

A dozen meanings, and only one answer. "Yes."

He drove into her, thrusting deep, and he swallowed her cry of pleasure.

With his mouth on hers she couldn't speak, couldn't tell him how good he felt moving inside her, how much she loved the way his hands stroked over her body, as if he couldn't stand leaving any part of her untouched. She couldn't tell him she wanted to spend every night in his bed, curled around his body with his heart thudding under her ear, a reminder that she never had to be alone again.

She couldn't tell him anything—and then his hands settled on her hips, lifting them until the angle of his strokes sparked fire in her blood and light behind her eyes, and she couldn't remember what she'd wanted to tell him.

She'd figure it out. Sometime between now and forever.

about the author

Kit Rocha is the pseudonym for co-writing team Donna Herren and Bree Bridges. After penning dozens of par-anormal novels, novellas and stories as Moira Rogers, they branched out into gritty, sexy dystopian romance.

The Beyond series has appeared on the New York Times and USA Today bestseller lists, and was honored with 2013 and 2017 RT Reviewer's Choice awards.

the beyond series

Beyond Shame
Beyond Control
Beyond Pain
Beyond Temptation
Beyond Jealousy
Beyond Solitude
Beyond Addiction
Beyond Possession
Beyond Innocence
Beyond Ruin
Beyond Ecstasy
Beyond Surrender

gideon's riders

Ashwin
Deacon
Ivan
Hunter

mercenary librarians

Deal With the Devil
The Devil You Know
Dance With the Devil

www.kitrocha.com